'My reputation i ~~already beyond~~ repair. What is a little more to gossip about?'

'You are the most infuriating woman. I am doing everything I can, and you are undoing it as fast as I try.'

Juliet tossed her head, her magnificent red hair flaring out in an arc of curls under the brim of her chip straw hat. 'You have gone too far this time, Brabourne. I will not marry you. After everything that has happened I would have thought you would be too embarrassed to even talk to my father, let alone ask for my hand.'

Sebastian's lip curled, but he was not amused. 'I am never embarrassed. That is something you will learn with time.'

Georgina Devon began writing fiction in 1985 and has never looked back. Alongside her prolific writing career, she has led an interesting life. Her father was in the United States Air Force, and after Georgina received her BA in Social Sciences from California State College, she followed her father's footsteps and joined the USAF. She met her husband, Martin, an A10 fighter pilot, while she was serving as an aircraft maintenance officer. Georgina, her husband and their young daughter now live in Tucson, Arizona, USA.

Look out for Lord Ravensford's story THE REBEL coming soon!

THE RAKE

Georgina Devon

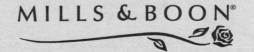

MILLS & BOON®

DID YOU PURCHASE THIS BOOK WITHOUT A COVER?

If you did, you should be aware it is **stolen property** as it was reported *unsold and destroyed* by a retailer. Neither the author nor the publisher has received any payment for this book.

All the characters in this book have no existence outside the imagination of the author, and have no relation whatsoever to anyone bearing the same name or names. They are not even distantly inspired by any individual known or unknown to the author, and all the incidents are pure invention.

All Rights Reserved including the right of reproduction in whole or in part in any form. This edition is published by arrangement with Harlequin Enterprises II B.V. The text of this publication or any part thereof may not be reproduced or transmitted in any form or by any means, electronic or mechanical, including photocopying, recording, storage in an information retrieval system, or otherwise, without the written permission of the publisher.

This book is sold subject to the condition that it shall not, by way of trade or otherwise, be lent, resold, hired out or otherwise circulated without the prior consent of the publisher in any form of binding or cover other than that in which it is published and without a similar condition including this condition being imposed on the subsequent purchaser.

MILLS & BOON and MILLS & BOON with the Rose Device are registered trademarks of the publisher.

First published in Great Britain 2000
Harlequin Mills & Boon Limited,
Eton House, 18-24 Paradise Road, Richmond, Surrey TW9 1SR

© Alison J. Hentges 2000

ISBN 0 263 82333 4

Set in Times Roman 10½ on 13 pt.
04-0101-58967

Printed and bound in Spain
by Litografia Rosés S.A., Barcelona

Chapter One

The morning sun barely peeked through the thick overhang of tree limbs. Green Park was still deserted at this time of morning. Not even the servants were about.

'Miss Juliet, you can no' be doing this,' Ferguson Coachman said sternly, his voice breaking the morning quiet.

Juliet Smythe-Clyde looked up between her thick cinnamon eyelashes while wiggling her toes in the too-large Hessians she had commandeered from her younger brother's wardrobe. She stamped her foot to try and better settle the heel. 'Rather this than for Papa to fight the Satanic Duke.'

The tall, spare coachman, his grey whiskers bristling about a narrow face, frowned. 'The master is a grown man. You are a slip of a girl and should no' be fighting his battles.'

'Enough,' Juliet said, slipping off the coat that

fitted her brother like a second skin and herself like a too-large nightrobe. 'Take this and fold it carefully. You know Harry will have an apoplexy if it gets wrinkled.'

Ferguson snorted, but carefully laid the coat on the seat of the dilapidated coach. Hobson, the butler, who was as round as he was majestic, presented the box holding two duelling pistols to his young mistress. Juliet reached for the one on the bottom.

'That one is primed and ready to go, miss,' Hobson said. 'I saw to it myself.'

Out of perversity, Juliet took the top one.

'That too is ready,' Hobson said, allowing himself a knowing smile which quickly disappeared. 'Stop this now, Miss Ju, while there is still time.'

Ferguson came to stand beside his crony, the two having become fast comrades despite the disparity in their stations. 'Have I no' been telling her the same since this began? She will no' listen to either of us.'

'I have to do this,' Juliet said, her voice cracking as the fear she had been holding at bay threatened to spill out of control. 'Someone must protect Papa from this latest folly.'

'Someone should no' be you, lass,' Ferguson retorted, his brogue thickening with anger and anxiety. 'You did no' tell the master to marry that doxy.'

'I promised Mama to care for Papa,' she whispered, the memory of her mother's dying request tightening her stomach. Mama was dead barely a year, yet Juliet remembered as if it had happened yesterday.

Mama had lain on the daybed in the morning room, the pale sunlight giving false colour to her shrunken cheeks. The illness that had eaten at her and kept her in constant pain had shrivelled her body and made Juliet secretly glad the end was near. She could not bear to see her beloved mama suffer so.

When Mama had beckoned her closer and begged her to care for Papa—flighty, irresponsible Papa— Juliet had promised. There had been nothing else she could do. She would have done anything to ease Mama's suffering. Anything. And someone had to watch over Papa once Mama was gone. Everyone knew that.

She sighed. She had not been able to keep Papa from marrying Mrs Winters, but she could keep him from throwing his life away for the woman. Surely not even the Duke of Brabourne would shoot to kill a young man who was only taking the place of the original dueller—would he?

Besides which, the Duke was at fault. Not she or Papa. The Duke was the one who had seduced another man's wife. As the one in error, he should delope. It was the honourable thing to do.

Juliet straightened her shoulders and sighted down the barrel of the pistol. At least growing up in the country had taught her something. She could shoot with the best of them, although Brabourne was said to be as deadly with a gun as he was with a sword and just as cold-hearted with either.

The sound of horses' hooves drew her attention. Three men stopped under a large oak some distance from Juliet's little group. All were dressed in great-coats and shiny Hessians with beaver hats perched rakishly atop their heads. She knew all by reputation and one by sight.

Dressed in man's garb, she had paid a very late-night visit to Lord Ravensford, one of Brabourne' seconds, four days before to tell him there was a change in plans. The duel needed to be moved forward. His lordship, too surprised by a puppy visiting him uninvited, had agreed to the change without argument, although his bronze brows had been raised in sardonic amusement during the entire conversation.

The other two men she had never seen. Lord Perth was said to be a rogue who went his own way, regardless of Society's rules. She guessed him to be the one who stood beside the bronze-haired Lord Ravensford. They were much of a height. She spared them little interest for they were not the person she was here to fight.

The third man jumped to the ground with a wiry grace that spoke of strength. She had heard the Duke was not only a rake but a Corinthian of the first stare. He was tall and lean, and when he shrugged out of his greatcoat and navy jacket, she noted his shoulders were broad in their stark white shirt, and his hips were narrow in their close-fitting breeches. His hair was as black as some said his heart was. His nose was a commanding jut of authority. She had heard his eyes were a deep blue, inherited from an Irish ancestor.

A *frisson* of something akin to fear, yet much more delicious, skittered down her spine. She turned away.

She gulped a deep breath of the cold air and wiped her damp palms along the sides of her breeches. For seconds she stared sightlessly at nothing and wondered if she would survive this encounter. It was a weakness she had not allowed herself before. She did not allow it for long now, either.

Lord Ravensford headed their way.

The rising sun glinted on his hair, making it look bright as a new-minted penny. There was a twinkle in his hazel eyes and a dimple in his square chin. He was a very fine-looking man.

'Well, puppy, where is Smythe-Clyde? You said he is the one who wanted this earlier meeting.'

Juliet felt a dull flush spread up her face only to recede. 'He…' she forced strength into her voice '…he is sick. Too sick to leave his bed. But honour demands that he meet Brabourne. So, as his second, I am taking his place.' She looked defiantly at Ravensford.

Ravensford glanced from her to the servants. A hint of disapproval tinged his words. 'Where is the other second? And where is the surgeon?'

'There is no other second, and Ferguson—' she gestured to the coachman '—is as good as any surgeon.'

'Havey-cavey.' Ravensford's gaze bored into Juliet. 'You are only a boy. There is not a chance that Brabourne will meet you. If Smythe-Clyde is too scared to follow through with this, then let him accept the dishonour.'

Juliet's hands clenched. 'I assure you, my lord, that my…that Smythe-Clyde is not afraid to meet the Duke. He is ill. Rather than draw this affair out, I am empowered to meet the Duke in Smythe-Clyde's place.'

Ravensford shook his head. 'I will pass on your words, but I doubt they will change anything.'

Without further discussion, the Earl turned away. Juliet sagged.

'Just as it should be,' Hobson said with smug satisfaction. 'Not even the greatest rakehell in all England would meet a mere boy on the field of honour. Especially when the quarrel is with another.'

Juliet had known from the beginning that the entire thing was far-fetched and likely to fail, but she'd had to try. Even now, as she saw Ravensford talk to the Duke, who looked her way, she knew she had to do something. Papa still intended to meet the

Duke at the original time, two days hence. Keeping
Papa from coming here then was the next hurdle
Juliet intended to face—after today's duel. One
thing at a time, she always told herself. Anything
could be accomplished if you did it one step at a
time.

Even from this distance, Juliet could see a scowl
mar the Duke's dark looks. The light breeze seemed
to carry his words.

'Smythe-Clyde is a coward and I refuse to meet
his stand-in.'

Panic shot through Juliet as the Duke turned from
Ravensford and reached for the coat he had just dis-
carded. She grabbed up one of the duelling pistols,
aimed and fired. The noise was loud in the still
morning. Splinters of wood exploded from the side
of the oak nearest Brabourne. Her adversary spun
around to face her.

Her bravado and the closeness of the shot froze
her to the ground. Not even the Duke's advance towards her released her paralysed muscles. With the
only part of her mind that still seemed to function,
Juliet noted the liquid power of his body as he
neared her. He stopped a scant foot from her shaking
body and razed her with the coldest blue eyes she
had ever seen.

'You are either an excellent shot or very lucky. I
don't know who you are, or why you feel compelled
to stand in for Smythe-Clyde, but the meeting be-

tween you and I is now personal. Whatever happens between us will have no bearing on the other. Do you understand me?'

His voice was as hard as his look, and yet the deep timbre did something to her insides that could only be described as exciting. Surely she was not going to fall under the legendary charms of one of England's greatest rakes? She had to wound him severely enough to keep him from meeting Papa, not swoon at his feet.

Juliet raised her chin up higher. 'I understand perfectly.'

'Good. Perth is going after a surgeon. We will wait upon their return to continue.'

Panic shot through Juliet. A surgeon would be fine if the Duke were the one injured. If she were, a surgeon would be a disaster.

'We do not need a sawbones, your Grace.'

His full bottom lip curved into a smile that was anything but friendly, yet did unnameable things to Juliet's breathing. 'You will need one, be sure of that.'

She blanched. 'Th…then Ferguson will do. He is better than anyone to be found in London.'

Brabourne's gaze flicked to the servant and back to Juliet. 'Your coachman.'

She nodded.

'Then it is on your head.'

He strode away before Juliet could respond. She

stared after him. He walked with a loose-limbed grace that flowed from his shoulders down to his narrow hips. She began to understand how her step-mother had succumbed to him. Even she, an innocent in spite of her three-and-twenty years, would be hard pressed to resist him if he pursued her. Not that he would. Not in a millenium. Not before today and especially not after today. Still, there was something incredibly attractive about him.

'Miss Juliet,' Hobson said, breaking into her ridiculous thoughts, 'best you use the gun I first recommended. It is bad luck to use the one already shot.'

'And I need all the luck I can get,' she murmured.

Ferguson stepped forward. 'Now, you remember what I said?'

She nodded. 'We meet, turn our backs to one another and walk twenty paces. Pivot and fire.'

She nodded again, worry gnawing at her nerves. Her jaw wanted to clench and her legs wanted to run away. Her stomach twisted into a knot and, if she had eaten anything before coming here she would be vomiting. Did men feel this way? She knew Brabourne did not.

'Now, Miss Juliet,' Hobson said softly.

Glancing at him, she saw the anxiety he felt for her. It made her hands shake more.

She did not look at the coachman, knowing she

would see the same fear in his eyes. Better to walk boldly forward and meet whatever fate held for her.

The pistol at her side, Juliet moved towards the approaching Duke. His black hair was tied back in a queue a style that was no longer in fashion, but then he was a rule unto himself. One strand had broken free. He ignored it, his attention on her.

Earlier she had seen and felt only the overwhelming sense of power he exuded...now she saw details. His brows winged over eyes the shade of indigo from which tiny lines radiated out, speaking of dissipation and long nights. The late-night growth of whiskers was black against his pale skin. His jaw was a firm line that belied the relaxed set of his shoulders.

He gave her a curt nod, and she knew it was time to turn and begin pacing. One, two...nineteen, twenty.

Juliet spun around, bringing her arm up as she moved. The pistol felt heavy and awkward. In spite of all her practice and determination, she wavered. It was one thing to plan on shooting a man. It was an entirely different thing to do so.

Brabourne had no such reservations.

A shot rang out in the still, quiet air. Juliet experienced a moment of surprise, followed by excruciating pain in her right shoulder. She crumbled to the ground, her pistol falling from unresponsive fingers.

He had shot her.

She brought her left hand up to the wound. Her fingers came away sticky. The metallic tang of blood pinched her nose. She felt herself losing consciousness and wondered if she would die.

'Here, here.' Ferguson fell to his knees beside her and waved smelling salts under her nose. 'This is no' the time to be passing out.'

Juliet nodded feebly. 'No. I have never fainted in my life. I shan't do so now.'

'That's my lass,' Ferguson said, probing gently at the wound.

A jolt like lightning twisted through Juliet. 'Ahh—that hurts,' she gasped.

Ferguson grunted. 'It will hurt much more before it gets better. The ball is lodged between muscle and bone. It must come out. You will be a while getting well.'

She gazed at him, knowing what he said and what it meant, but not wanting to believe him. 'How will I keep this from Papa? I cannot stay in my room unattended even for a day. He will need me. The staff will need me.'

Hobson was on her other side. 'You should have thought of those things before starting this hare-brained escapade, miss.'

'I thought he would delope,' she said softly, wincing as Ferguson probed deeper. 'He...' She gasped as fresh pain seared her. 'He is the one at fault, not Papa. Not me.'

Dark spots danced in her vision. 'The smelling salts,' she whispered.

The two servants exchanged glances. Better to let her faint. She would not feel the pain.

'Is something vital severed?' the Duke of Brabourne said from where he had stopped to watch the situation. 'If the puppy had maintained a side profile instead of squaring completely around, the ball would have grazed the flesh of his upper arm. I did not shoot to kill him.'

'Thank you for that, your Grace,' Hobson said, never taking his attention off Juliet.

'Don't thank me for something I did for myself. If the boy dies, I must flee to the Continent,' Brabourne said. 'That does not suit my plans at the moment.'

Ferguson snorted in disgust.

'You understand perfectly,' Brabourne said. 'Now, what is the prognosis?'

'He's lost a fair amount of blood, and I do no' ken if I can get the ball out here. I can stop most of the bleeding.'

Ravensford, who had come up, looked down. 'You had better get the lad home, then. We will send the surgeon to your direction.'

Juliet listened to the men talking, their words seeming to come through a long tunnel, but at the mention of going home she forced her eyes open. 'Ca…cannot go home. No surgeon. No one know.'

The effort to talk made her feel even more light-headed. She tried to sit up, but found she could not.

'Do no' fash yerself, lad,' Ferguson said. He pressed a makeshift bandage to the wound, trying to staunch the flow of blood.

'What did he mean, not go home?' Ravensford asked.

Hobson, who had gone to the carriage for the laudanum he had packed just in case, returned and said, 'Just that, my lord. The lad cannot go home.'

Brabourne eyed the butler. 'Surely you jest. What type of family does the boy have that he cannot go home?'

Hobson stoically met the Duke's gaze. 'The young master cannot go to the London house in this condition. We will convey him to the country estate.'

Juliet tightened her grip on the butler's hand. 'I must be bandaged so none will know. I cannot stay from home long. You know that.'

Ferguson, tried beyond his patience, said, 'You will do as we tell you.'

Juliet frowned. 'I will do as I must.'

'How far away is the estate?' Brabourne asked.

'Half a day, your Grace,' Hobson said.

'That is much too far, Brabourne,' Ravensford said quietly. 'The wound does not look fatal now, but the continued loss of blood could make it so.' He met his friend's gaze. 'You cannot afford that. Only six months ago you nearly did away with Williams in a sword fight. Prinny will not be so lenient with you if this boy dies.'

Brabourne smoothed one winged brow. 'You must take the puppy to his London house. There is nothing else to be done.'

Ferguson paused in his ministrations to look up at the Duke. 'I will no' do that, your Grace. The lad is right in saying that no one must know what has happened.'

Brabourne looked hard at the servant and spoke softly. 'Are you telling me no?'

Ferguson swallowed hard. 'Yes, your Grace, that be what I'm telling you.'

'And you?' Brabourne pinned Hobson with his gaze.

The butler's ruddy complexion blanched. 'I must stand by Ferguson, your Grace.'

Brabourne looked at Ravensford. The Earl shrugged.

'What is the boy's secret?' Brabourne demanded.

The two servants looked long at one another. Hobson made the Duke a bow. 'The young master met you today without anyone knowing, except us. Lord Smythe-Clyde still plans on meeting you in two days. Master Ju was hoping that by duelling

with you today you would consider it finished and
not be here when his lordship comes.'

'Stupid.' Brabourne shook his head.

'Misguided,' Ravensford murmured.

Juliet groaned as much from having her plan revealed and hearing how inadequate it sounded when
spoken as from pain. Everyone's attention snapped
back to her.

'Enough,' Ferguson said. 'Hobson, help me carry
the young master to the carriage. We must be on our
way if we hope to get him to Richmond before he
has lost too much blood.'

'Ravensford?' Brabourne looked at his friend.

Ravensford put one well-manicured hand up as
though to ward off a blow. 'Not me, Brabourne. Nowhere does it say a second's duty is to house a
wounded opponent.'

Brabourne's lips thinned before forming a small
smile. 'As usual, Ravensford, you are correct. I suppose if I don't want the boy to die on me I shall
have to make arrangements for his shelter. It is apparent his servants are misguided in their loyalty.'
He turned to the men who were in the process of
depositing the youth in the coach. 'Take the boy to
my town house.' He cast a wicked glance at his
friend. 'Ravensford will direct the surgeon to my
address.'

Ravensford made a mocking bow. The two servants exchanged horrified looks. Their charge lay

limply on the cushions, having passed out when lifted.

'Is something amiss?' Brabourne enquired at his haughtiest.

Ferguson climbed out of the coach and made the Duke a bow. 'Nothing, your Grace. If you will give me directions, we will go there immediately. But we have no need of a surgeon. A clean knife, hot water and plenty of bandages will be enough.'

'Be sure you do not need help before turning it away,' Brabourne said quietly. 'I do not intend to have the boy die.'

'Neither do I, your Grace.' Ferguson stood his ground in spite of the discomfort that had him twisting his hands.

'Then follow me,' Brabourne ordered.

Minutes later, he, Ravensford and Perth cantered from the shelter of the trees, the lumbering coach close behind.

'I hope you do not live to regret this day's work,' Ravensford said.

'So do I, my friend.' Brabourne cast one last look over his shoulder. 'So do I.'

Chapter Two

Sebastian FitzPatrick, Duke of Brabourne, frowned down at his unwanted guest. The boy's milk-white skin was covered in cinnamon freckles. Hair the colour of a sunset tangled around the sweep of cheekbone and curve of brow. There was a tight look around the eyes, as though the youth were in pain even though he slept. He probably was. It had taken time and considerable digging to extract the ball. He had lost a fair amount of blood during the ordeal and would be weak for some time.

A chair scraped behind Sebastian. 'Can I be helpin', your Grace?'

Sebastian glanced back at the coachman whose head had been nodding seconds before. Ferguson was the man's name. 'Has your master regained consciousness?'

'No, your Grace.'

'Have you eaten or had any sleep?'

'No, your Grace.'

'Then do so.'

'Beggin' your pardon, your Grace, but I must stay with the master.'

'One of my servants will do as well. Now go.' Sebastian returned his scrutiny to the boy.

He was as frail as a willow and with a hint of lavender about him, a strange scent for a man. Full lips the colour of pomegranates gave him an effeminate air. And yet the youth had fought him in a duel. He had put his life at stake for another person. Sebastian would not do so, and was sure he did not know anyone who would, with a few exceptions— Ravensford and Perth. Perhaps that was the fascination this boy had over him, the reason he found himself in this room gazing down at a person he did not even know. He reached out to touch the boy's brow.

The servant cleared his throat.

Sebastian's hand dropped to his side. 'Haven't you gone yet?' he asked without turning around.

'I can no' be leavin' my charge…your Grace.'

Irritation chewed at Sebastian. 'I told you that one of my servants will stand watch.'

The servant made a sound very much like choking. 'Beggin' yer pardon, your Grace, but I canna trust the young master to someone unknown.'

Sebastian lowered his voice to a silky thread. 'You are stubborn and forthright for a servant.' The coachman stood his ground even though his gaze lowered deferentially. 'Then I shall stay with your charge. Surely that will meet your requirement.' In the silence that followed, Sebastian heard the man gulp.

'I must no' leave his side.'

'Are you afraid I will do something to your precious charge? I have plenty of vices, but I assure you that molesting boys is not one of them.'

Ferguson whitened, but spoke around his obvious discomfort. 'I am well aware of your Grace's pastimes.'

His patience suddenly gone, Sebastian spun around. *'Get out now.'* Still the servant hesitated. Sebastian wondered what kind of master the boy must be to engender such loyalty in his people. 'If you do not leave, I shall have you thrown bodily from the room. When your master awakens, I wish to speak privately with him. In the meantime, I will watch him and have my housekeeper provide anything needed. I don't want him dead any more than you do.'

Still the servant stayed. Sebastian strode to the fireplace and reached for the velvet cord above the mantel.

'Ferguson…' a weak voice came from the bed '…do as his Grace says. I will be all right.'

'I'll no' be leavin' you with the likes of his Grace.'

This loyalty was vastly interesting, but Sebastian was not known for his patience. 'Get out now, before I finish what I started and have my footmen throw you out.'

The boy struggled to sit and the servant rushed to his side. 'No, you should no' be doing this.' The coachman fussed like a mother hen.

'Go,' the boy said. 'If the Duke wanted to hurt me, he would have...' He took laboured breaths, his cheeks flushing and then paling. 'He would have aimed to kill.'

'You ken why I can no' leave,' Ferguson muttered under his breath.

Sebastian had excellent hearing, but said nothing. There was something amiss here, and he was beginning to see what it might be. There was a delicacy to the youth's wrist when he lifted it to pat the servant's gnarled hand. Sebastian's mouth twisted. He was a fool not to have seen it earlier, but the puppy's bravery had blinded him.

The boy whispered, 'You will only make him more suspicious by insisting.' Raising his voice, the youth said, 'Now go. You may come back as soon as his Grace is done questioning me. Please.'

Ferguson gave the Duke a threatening look, but did as ordered. The door closed behind the servant with a defiant snap.

Sebastian noted the dark circles under the girl's gold-flecked hazel eyes, for girl she was. Now that he knew, it was obvious. He was a connoisseur of women and knew that her lashes, the colour of honey sable and just as thick as that fine fur, would be the envy of any courtesan. As would the lush, burnt red curls that lay like flames on the pillow. For a moment he wondered if her temper matched her hair and if her passion matched her determination. It would be interesting to find out—but not now.

'Why are you impersonating a boy?' he asked without preamble.

She paled even more, but her voice was defiant. 'You are addled from too much dissipation, your Grace.'

He smiled slowly, his gaze running boldly over her, enjoying her bravado. 'Not at the moment. Now that I look beyond your dress…and actions, it is obvious you are a woman.' He ignored her snort. 'Probably with your breasts bound and the borrowed finery of a male family member. Since I have never had your acquaintance foisted on me, you haven't been presented to Society, although you speak and carry yourself like Quality. I would imagine you have lived your life in the country and have only recently come to town.'

She stared baldly at him. For a long moment, Sebastian thought she would continue to deny her true gender.

With a sigh of weariness, she sank back into the pillow. 'But, how...? You did not suspect before...?'

Sebastian smiled, a rare one of enjoyment that softened the hard angles of his face. He reached for the hand nearest him, realised it was on her wounded side before touching her and stretched across her instead. He caught her fingers even as she started to slide them under the covers.

Leaning over her, he brought her captured hand towards him, but not so near as to force her on to her wounded shoulder. He turned the palm up.

'Your skin is soft as velvet and unblemished. Your nails are short but well cared for. No sun has touched you to toughen or darken your complexion.' One by one, he examined her fingers. 'Long and elegant. A lady's hands. Certainly not those of a man.'

With that inherent need to charm and seduce that made him the successful rake he was, he brought her hand to his lips. She yanked back as though bitten. He let her go.

'Why did you meet me?'

She met his eyes openly even as her body sagged visibly with exhaustion. 'I had to. Someone had to stand up to you.' Her voice was weak, but a thread of determination ran through it.

Sebastian found himself taken aback by her ve-hemence. 'Stand up to me?'

The hand of her wounded arm lay flaccid. Her

other hand clenched the fine linen sheet. 'You are a libertine and a dangerous, amoral man in a position of power that has allowed you to do as you pleased.'

A glint of admiration for her courage lit his eyes, only to be doused by an emotion Sebastian had long ago decided would not rule him. She spoke only the truth. 'And what of it? I am not the only one of my ilk.'

'I know,' she muttered. 'But you are the only one of your kind to impact on my family.'

'Ah,' he said mildly, his reactions once more under control. 'Your family. What is Smythe-Clyde to you? An uncle, cousin, father?'

Her skin, which he had thought pale as milk, took on the translucent clarity of the moon. With the right clothing she would be a beauty; a very unusual one, but a beauty none the less. Beautiful women intrigued him—for a while.

She turned away from him. Her chest laboured. 'It is none of your business.'

'A lover, perhaps?'

Her head whipped back and there was such anger in her that he found his interest increasing. When one could have anything one wanted, a challenge was not to be ignored. Particularly one with such possibilities.

'You are perverted,' she breathed.

He pulled the nearest chair to the edge of the bed and lounged back into it. 'No, merely curious.'

He found himself fascinated by the way colour played across her cheeks, only to flee and return again later. Her lips compressed into a thin line, then opened like a fine rose when heated by the sun.

She sighed. 'It is none of your business, and I am too tired to continue arguing with you.'

He could see by the deepening of lines around her eyes and mouth that she spoke the truth. 'This is a delicious game we play, my sweet, but you are right, you have not the strength for it.'

Her face tightened. The angle of cheek and jaw sharpened. But she said nothing.

He studied her a while longer. 'I can always make enquiries about Smythe-Clyde's family. I assure you it will not take my secretary long to find out more.'

Her body stiffened. 'Why are you doing this?'

'Because you are a mystery, and mysteries beg to be solved.'

'A mystery. Something to entertain you, not a person.'

He nodded his head in curt acceptance of her hit. 'Exactly. What is Smythe-Clyde to you?'

Her chin lifted. 'My father. Now will you leave me alone?'

The answer was not what he had expected. 'For now.'

Not only was the girl foolhardy, she was reckless. As the daughter of a baron, she would be completely ruined if word of her escapade got out. Well-brought-up young ladies did not even know about duelling, let alone participate in one. Worse, if rumour reached the *ton* that she was in his house, in one of his beds, Society would try to force him to marry her. The girl had to go.

Long minutes went by as they met each other's gaze. The clock on the mantel chimed eight. A knock on the door signalled interruption.

He rose with languid grace and crossed to the closed curtains of the window before saying, 'Enter.'

Juliet sagged in relief when Ferguson entered carrying a tray. Exhaustion, pain and fear ate at her. What would Brabourne do now that he knew she was a woman? Would he denounce her to the world?

She glanced over to see him watching her with a brooding intensity that did nothing to calm her frayed nerves. He was dressed for evening. Perhaps Almack's, although she doubted that he frequented that very respectable Marriage Mart. More likely he was headed out to one of his clubs, to be followed by dalliance with one of his many female companions. At least this time it would not be with her stepmother.

Still, he was the most handsome man she had ever seen. The perfect cut of his black coat showed broad shoulders to advantage. Black pantaloons hugged narrow hips, and white stockings revealed impeccable calves. His cravat was tied in what she as-

sumed was the Brabourne Soirée, an arrangement
her younger brother had yet to be successful dupli-
cating, although Harry tried repeatedly. But all Brabourne's sartorial elegance was nothing compared to
the man himself.

He took her breath away. Or, more probably, she
told herself, it was her wound making her think air
was in short supply. His unfashionably long hair
waved over his collar like a raven's wing, moving
with every step he took. His eyes were brilliantly
blue and penetrating. Too penetrating, she thought,
as a blush heated her flesh. And his mouth. She had
only seen lips like his on the marble face of a Greek
god. His male beauty—for there was really no other
word to describe how he looked—was marred only
by a look of bored dissipation that hovered around
his eyes and mouth.

She was more than thankful he had no interest in
her, for she did not think she could resist him if he
wanted her. Better for all of them if she left immediately. Ferguson would see to it. He should have
taken her to her father's country house in the first
place.

'Here, young master,' Ferguson said, setting the
tray down on the table near the bed.

The scent of chicken broth made Juliet's mouth
water. She tried to sit up, but after a feeble attempt
fell back. The exertion made her voice a thin reed.

'There is no need for the pretence, Ferguson. His Grace knows I am a woman.'

Ferguson's hand, with a spoon of broth, paused halfway between bowl and patient. He cast the Duke a fulminating look.

'Don't worry,' the Duke drawled, 'I will resist the urge to ravish her. But you had best see to it that no one else realises her deception.' His eyes gleamed wickedly. 'I cannot control everyone who works for me.'

'Yes, your Grace,' Ferguson said, frowning down at Juliet. 'I will have the lass out of here before anyone is the wiser.'

'That would be best,' her reluctant host said, going to the door. He looked back at her once, then left. The door closed softly behind him.

Tension Juliet hadn't felt rushed out, and she sank further into the softness of the feather bed. 'As soon as I've eaten we must leave.'

Ferguson nodded. 'Hobson will be back shortly to see how you do, lass. I will fetch the coach while he is here.'

Tenderly, he propped her up on the full pillows and helped her eat the broth. Juliet was glad of his help since her hand refused to be steady. When she finished her head fell back.

'I am so tired, Ferguson. I think I will sleep. Waken me when Hobson arrives.'

'Yes, lass.' He poured a generous portion of laudanum into a glass and added water to blunt the bitter taste of the medicine. 'Take this. It will help ye sleep and ease the discomfort.'

Ju smiled weakly. 'I do not need it to sleep, but it would be nice to have less pain.' She swallowed the concoction with a grimace.

Ferguson settled her comfortably, noting that she fell asleep before he reached his chair. She was a good, brave lass. Headstrong and not much accomplished in feminine things, but a good girl.

Sebastian lifted his hand and a waiter rushed over. 'Another bottle of port.'

'Immediately, your Grace.' The servant hurried away.

'This is our sixth bottle,' Ravensford said. He tunnelled long, white fingers through his thick red hair. He had a smile and a way about him that could charm the chemise off a doxy without a penny changing hands.

'Then we are four behind,' Jason Beaumair, Earl of Perth, said. He was wickedly handsome, with the blackest eyes set in a narrow face, which was framed in equally black hair frosted at the temples and forehead. A scar ran from his right eyebrow to the corner of his mouth. It was said he had received it in a duel over another man's wife.

Sebastian gazed at his friends. If Jonathan, Marquis of Langston, were here, they would be complete. But Langston had married the famous actress, Samantha Davidson, and was an infrequent visitor to White's now.

'We need one more for whist,' Sebastian said, pouring from the newly arrived bottle of port.

A flurry of words, followed by the thud of a table hitting the floor, drew Sebastian's attention. A boy—or young man—was wrestling his way into the room. The youth had a narrow face and carrot-red hair. His hazel eyes were wild and angry. Freckles marched across his prominent nose, looking as though a cook had sprinkled nutmeg on his skin.

His gaze came to rest on Sebastian. Fierce satisfaction curled the boy's lips into a snarl. 'Release me!' he demanded, twisting out of a servant's grasp. He strode to Sebastian's table.

Sebastian took in the look of the cub and knew instantly who he was related to. In a bored tone, he said, 'A Smythe-Clyde.'

'Harold Jacob Smythe-Clyde.' The boy stood defiantly, hands on hips.

Sebastian groaned inwardly. First the chit and now this. And all because of Emily Winters. The former Mrs Winters was getting the cut direct the next time he had the misfortune to meet her, and the girl was leaving as soon as he returned home.

He propped one well-shod foot on the table and lounged back to look up at Harold Jacob Smythe-Clyde. 'You are not invited to join us,' he drawled.

The boy drew himself up. 'I did not come to game with scum such as yourself…your Grace.'

Sebastian raised one dark brow. He sensed both Ravensford and Perth tensing. To ease them he waved one languid white hand. 'Then begone. You are a bore.'

'And you, sir, are a libertine, a rake and a seducer of innocent women.' The furious words fell into a dearth of sound. Red rose up the boy's cheeks and spread to his ears. But he held his ground.

The tic at Sebastian's right eye started. He focused on the cut of his shoe. 'You tread dangerous ground,' he said softly.

'I challenge you to a duel. Weapons of your choosing.' If the boy's voice trembled, it was barely noticeable.

'I do not stoop to duel with halfwits.' Sebastian reached for his glass and took a long drink of the strong wine. This family was becoming unacceptable.

'You, your Grace, are a bastard. I know how you—'

In one smooth movement, Sebastian rose to his feet. He planted a facer on the boy that knocked the cub to the floor. 'No one calls me a bastard,' he said quietly, dangerously. 'Now get out of here before I run you through where you stand.'

He poured out the remainder of the bottle and downed it in one long swallow. 'It is time we left,' he said, his gaze sweeping over his friends. 'White's has lost its exclusivity.'

Before the boy could get to his feet, Sebastian and his friends left. The hour was early yet, and St James's was crowded with people.

'Another puppy after your blood,' Perth said in his dark, deep voice. 'Smythe-Clyde must have been busy in his youth.'

'My understanding,' Ravensford said, swinging his gold-tipped cane nonchalantly, 'is that the baron has only one son.' He smiled at Sebastian. 'And you just laid him out with an upper cut that Jackson himself would have admired.'

Sebastian settled his beaver hat at a devilish angle. 'That is high praise coming from someone Jackson cannot defeat in the ring.' He glanced around. 'But enough. Shall we head for Annabell's? There is more to life than wine and gaming.'

'So true,' Perth drawled, falling into step. 'There is wine, gaming and women.'

'Particularly women,' Ravensford said with a devilish gleam in his eyes.

Chapter Three

In the small hours of the morning, Sebastian strolled into the room where his unwelcome guest stayed. The two servants hovered around the bed, muttering direly. The Duke did not like the tension he sensed.

'What is the matter?' Sebastian asked, striding to the group.

Hobson looked up, his round face creased with worry. 'Miss Juliet is worse.'

Sebastian looked at the patient. Her face was flushed. The nightshirt he had loaned her lay damply against her neck and shoulder. Her hands fluttered like trapped butterflies. Irritation mingled with concern, making his brows dip inward.

'Is her wound inflamed?'

Ferguson looked up from where he was gently taking the bandage off. 'I believe so, your Grace.'

The skin where the ball had entered was swollen and red, with streaks of crimson starting to form.

Her eyes opened and their sparkling gaze alighted on Sebastian.

'Brabourne,' she muttered, the words slurred but recognisable. 'A man's nemesis and a woman's heart's desire.' She giggled, only to end in a gasp of pain as Ferguson tried to clean the seeping wound. 'Blast! Must you be so clumsy?' she gasped.

They were the last coherent words she said as Hobson tipped a glass of water and laudanum down her throat.

'I need to make a poultice,' Ferguson said, laying aside the cloth he had used to sponge her shoulder. He looked at the Duke.

Sebastian almost sighed as he felt the noose of involvement tightening around his neck. It was obvious the chit could not be moved. 'And what do you expect from me?'

'You are supposed to have one of the best stables in the country, your Grace. I am sure your head groom has what I need.'

'You mean to put the same poultice on your mistress that you would use for a horse?'

Ferguson shrugged. 'It works for four-legged creatures. Why not two-legged ones?'

Sebastian had no better suggestion since they would not allow a doctor, which he thoroughly agreed with now that he knew the circumstances. 'Go and tell Jenkins that you have my permission to use whatever you need.'

The one servant left and, with a resignation that tightened his gut, Sebastian turned to the other. 'And what do you need?'

Hobson glanced up. 'More cool water would help, your Grace. Miss Juliet is raging hot; no matter how much I sponge her, she only seems to burn the more.'

Sebastian moved to the bellpull over the mantel only to stop before summoning a servant. His brooding glance settled on the girl. With her flushed cheeks and swollen lips, no one could mistake her for anything but what she was. If someone were still so unobservant as to think she was male, the swell of her breasts under the shirt and single sheet would be enough to enlighten them. One of the first things she had done after he had pierced her disguise had been to remove the binding from her breasts so she could breathe better and lie more comfortably.

This situation was becoming more and more complicated. The very last thing he needed was for word of his unwanted guest's real identity to leak out. At three and thirty, Sebastian had no intentions of marrying someone not of his choosing. Not even if some foolish chit's reputation depended upon him wedding her.

Nor did he want the world to know he had shot a woman. It was bad enough that he knew. Damn her for putting him in this dishonourable position.

He pulled the bell and moved quickly into the

hall. A footman appeared instantly, impeccably dressed in the Duke's black and green colours.

'Fetch Mrs Burroughs,' Sebastian instructed.

The young man's eyes widened, but he bowed and left.

Sebastian had a rule that servants who worked during the day would not be expected to work at night. That went particularly for his housekeeper and butler, whom he knew laboured fourteen and sixteen hours a day. Never before had he summoned Mrs Burroughs from her bed. He did not intend ever to do so again.

He stepped back into the sickroom. Mrs Burroughs would knock, and he did not intend for anyone else to hear their discussion.

Juliet Smythe-Clyde looked no better. Hobson's worried frown was deeper. 'Ferguson knows what he's about,' the butler mumbled, as though to reassure himself.

'If he does not, then we are going to have problems,' Sebastian stated. 'I have no intentions of fleeing to the Continent. Nor do I intend for anyone to discover your mistress's whereabouts.'

A discreet knock stopped the butler from saying whatever was on the tip of his tongue. Instead he turned back to his charge.

Sebastian crossed to the door and asked, 'Mrs Burroughs?'

'Yes, m'lord.'

He let her in, quickly closing the door behind her. 'We have a problem.'

She looked from him to the bed. Her iron-coloured brows shot up, wrinkling her forehead into a dozen creases. Her mouth puckered in dismay and then disapproval. ''Twould seem we do, *your Grace*.' Her emphasis on his title told him more clearly than words that she was shocked and unhappy with the situation.

He looked at the old woman who had started service with his father over thirty-two years ago. She had been his nanny. When he'd inherited the title, he had retired his parents' housekeeper and appointed Mrs Burroughs. She was not a woman who would have taken well to retirement.

'You are the only person I can trust with this information. We must nurse her until she is able to be moved. And no one must find out.'

She snorted. 'I would hope my husband can be trusted with this, your Grace. 'Twill take more than the three of us here to give the girl round-the-clock care. I have a house to run, I'm sure this gentleman here has duties, and you have all of London to carouse through.'

The disapproval in her voice when she described his activities was softened by the affection in her brown eyes. She did not like the life he led, but she cared for him.

Hobson, realising that Mrs Burroughs had a sensible head on her shoulders, moved closer. 'I am the butler to Miss Juliet's father and I cannot be gone much.'

Her knowing gaze went from Hobson to the girl. 'A secret. Well, his Grace was always one for getting into scrapes.'

Ferguson's return from the stables saved Sebastian from needing to comment. There were times he regretted making his nanny his housekeeper.

Ferguson set about applying the poultice.

Late the next afternoon, Sebastian sat at table breaking his fast. Soon he would have to take up his post with the patient. Ferguson had returned to Smythe-Clyde's house after rebandaging the shoulder. Hobson had stayed until Mrs Burroughs could find time in the late morning hours. Burroughs had been in and out. From the surreptitious glances the footman was sending his way, Sebastian knew the servants wondered what was going on.

'Your Grace.' One of the footmen bowed and presented a silver tray on which lay a white calling card with the corner bent.

Sebastian picked it up and read the name Harold Jacob Smythe-Clyde, his unwelcome charge's brother. 'I am not at home.'

'Yes, my lord.'

Minutes later, the sound of a raised voice reached

Sebastian. It was followed by the closing of the front door. This family was nothing but trouble.

With a sigh, Sebastian rose. How had he let himself get into this predicament? He was a man who had always considered his own comforts first.

First it had been to keep the girl's servants from taking her into the country and possibly threatening her life. Then it had been because she was too sick to be moved.

In an unconscious gesture, he smoothed his left eyebrow with one finger. Now he allowed the chit to stay here because she needed to regain some strength before returning home. In her present condition it would not be long before someone realised she was hurt. Then the duel would come out, and her stay here. That would ruin her. Her courage intrigued him and he did not want to see her pay for it. Too few people of his acquaintance had her strength.

In spite of all that, respectable young women of the *ton* did not spend nights under any man's roof, let alone his. His reputation as a rake did not bear scrutiny. Even he, as immune as he was to Society's dictates, would be hard pressed to refuse marriage if it were ever discovered that the girl had spent several nights under his roof. She had to leave. Soon.

In the meantime, he would amuse himself at Tattersall's. There was a fine filly that had caught his

eye last week. Spirited and headstrong, the horse
reminded him of his unwanted guest. At least with
the animal he could determine whether he wanted
her in his stable.

Juliet roused from a nightmare where Papa
duelled with Brabourne and was hit. Moisture
beaded her brow and her night shirt clung to her
skin. Why was she so hot?

Where was she?

The sound of someone lightly snoring caught her
attention. A long, lithe man sprawled in one of two
chairs, his legs spread out and seeming to go on for
ever. A wave of dark hair shadowed his sallow
cheeks and gave him a demonic cast.

Memory returned.

She rolled to one side and pushed up with her
good arm. Pain shot through her bad shoulder. She
gasped and squeezed her eyes shut against unwanted
tears.

'What the deuce are you about?'

She turned her head and stared straight up at him.
Without her hearing him he had come to the bed.
His black brows were drawn and his blue eyes shot
sparks.

'I am trying to sit up,' she said peevishly, wishing
she did not hurt so much. 'Why else would I be
twisting around?'

'Whining does not become you,' he stated baldly,

the lines between his brows easing. 'Let me help you or you will undo all the good work your coachman has done.'

Without waiting for her reply, he reached down and hooked a hand under each of her arms and hauled her up on to the pillows. Another gasp of pain escaped her and once more tears welled in her eyes. She told herself that her blurred vision gave her the impression his face held contrition. There was no doubt in her mind that he found her a nuisance rather than someone he might be concerned over.

Long moments passed and his hands stayed on her. His warmth flowed into her, increasing her fever and making her pulse jump. No man had ever touched her so intimately. Juliet looked up at him and felt herself blushing.

He finally released her. 'Is that better?' he asked, his voice hoarse as though he had a cold.

She nodded. Strange sensations coursed through her body, and for a weak moment she wished he would touch her again. She was a fool.

'Would you like some water?'

'Yes,' she muttered. 'Please. I am so hot. It is like a furnace in here.'

He poured the liquid and held it to her lips. 'You are feverish. The wound is inflamed and Ferguson has been treating it with horse poultices.'

Juliet chuckled. 'That is very like him. Has it helped?'

He set the empty glass on a stand. 'It seems so. This is the first time since last night that you have been awake and coherent at the same time.'

Her eyes widened. 'Surely you jest?'

'Not about this.' He turned away and fetched the chair he had been sprawled in. He set it near the bed and sank into its thick leather cushions.

'I suppose not,' she said, looking away from his intense perusal. 'I cannot suppose I am the kind of woman you would choose to be in one of your beds.' As soon as the words were out, she realised how provocative they were. 'I...I did not mean that the way it sounded.'

He raised one brow. 'You did not? How disappointing.'

She had thought herself warm before, but now she flamed.

A slow smile cut a line into his cheek. It was seductive in the intensity it gave to his face, as though he were truly interested in her as a woman. Part of her wanted to melt. A larger part wanted to run. He was a dangerous man for a woman to be around.

'I am sure there are many women eager to share one of your beds and that none of them would be here from wounds.' The words came out like an accusation instead of the reasonable statement of fact she had intended. He was a disturbing man.

'True, but then they would be boring. You, I'd wager, are never boring.'

She had a sense that he was flirting with her. She looked away from his unsettling scrutiny and her fingers plucked at the sheet without her being aware of what she did.

'Anyone can be boring,' she finally whispered.

'So I have generally found,' he replied drily. 'But then no other woman has ever fought me in a duel. Nor has any other woman told me she could not go home and then convinced me to let her stay in mine. Why wouldn't your family help hide your condition?'

The abrupt change of subject surprised her. It was as though he had been trying to trick her into answering him, but there was no secret. 'Harry would have. Poor Papa would have run to his new wife and expected her to handle everything. I don't trust my stepmother. Everything she does is designed to further her own ends. She would be furious.'

'Because you fought a duel or because you tried to take your father's place?'

'Both.'

'Would she have hit you?' His eyes darkened as he waited for her answer. 'Would your father?'

'No,' she squeaked, shocked that he could even think such a thing. 'Papa has never hit us. Mama was always the one to discipline us. She or our nurse, and later our governess and tutor. My stepmother would not dare.'

His mouth tightened. 'Did you see much of your mother?'

A soft smile of memory lit Juliet's face. 'Yes. Always. Mama was a curate's daughter, and she believed children were a gift to be treasured.'

'A nice fancy,' he said, bitterness making the words hard and brittle.

No emotion showed on his face. It was as though he had shut his real self behind a mask. The urge to ask him why was great, but Juliet hesitated. He was not a man who invited closeness or questions about himself.

He stood so sharply that his chair tottered on its back legs before settling down. He paced to the fireplace, grabbed the poker and jabbed viciously at the already roaring fire.

Juliet saw pain in the tense set of his shoulders. The longing to comfort him was great, but she sensed that to say something would only make him draw further into himself. Instead, she waited quietly for him to make the next overture. She did not wait long.

He put the poker back and strode to the bed, where he grabbed the chair and repositioned it in its original place. 'I will send Mrs Burroughs to help you change into a fresh shirt. But first tell me why your father's anger kept you from going home when you knew he would not punish you.'

She smiled ruefully. He would not give confidences, but he expected them of others. Still, it would do no harm. 'I could not have kept my condition hidden from Papa. When he found out, he would have been angry with me because he would have been hurt that I felt he needed to be protected. That I did not trust him to take care of himself. Although everyone will tell you that he cannot.'

'A grown man cannot take care of himself?' the Duke asked in disbelief. 'I think you exaggerate.'

'Not about Papa. He can find his way anywhere in the country, but he is forever becoming lost here in London. Just as he will misplace every one of the twelve pairs of glasses I have got for him. Or reach his hand into a lion's cage because he is curious about what the creature will do.' She gave a long-suffering sigh.

The Duke chuckled. 'A handful.'

'Always. At first I was thrilled that he was remarrying, even though it was not yet a year after Mama's death. But then…' She clamped her mouth shut on the words. In a falsely brisk voice, she stated, 'But that is neither here nor there. You are right, your Grace. A clean nightshirt would be most welcome.'

He made her a mocking bow before leaving. She had no doubt he knew exactly what she had stopped herself from saying. After all, he was the man her stepmother was having an affair with. He would know the woman. Just the thought made her chest tighten, and the wound she had nearly forgotten started to ache anew.

How long would it take her to learn to protect herself against his charm? Probably for ever, said a tiny voice she wanted to ignore.

Sebastian sprawled across the large leather wing-back, his right leg indecorously thrown over the chair's arm. He swung his foot, the evening pump catching the firelight. He twirled the half-full glass of whisky before taking a long swallow. The liquor burned down his throat. He smiled grimly. The savageness of the liquid matched the emotions running through him.

'Damned uncivilised drink,' he muttered, taking another gulp. He would probably consume the entire decanter. He had got a taste for it from his friend Jonathan, Marquis of Langston, who had learned about it from his younger brother, Lord Alastair St Simon.

The chit had to go. The only thing worse than having her continued presence in his home would be to have her die while occupying one of his beds. She had already been here two days and was on her second night. But she was out of danger, or nearly so. And she was a distraction.

He emptied his glass.

A knock caught his attention as he rose to pour more whisky. 'Who is it?' he demanded, moving to his desk and emptying the contents of the decanter into his glass.

'Your Grace,' Burroughs, the butler, intoned, entering the room and closing the door behind himself. His long, rather bulbous nose rose several inches, a pose Sebastian knew the man assumed when his sensibilities were affronted.

'There is a *person* to see you.'

Sebastian raised one black brow. 'A *person*?'

Burroughs puffed up his ample girth. 'A woman…as your Grace very well knows.'

Which one of his lady-friends would be so lost to propriety as to visit him here? Sebastian neither cared nor knew. He drank the whisky in one gulp. 'Tell her I am not at home.'

Burroughs bowed, a smile of approval making his round face glow. 'My pleasure, your Grace.'

Sebastian set the empty glass on the corner of his desk and decided it was time for bed. Most of London was asleep, and only his irritation at having his home pose a threat to his peace of mind had kept him up this late.

Sounds of a scuffle barely preceded the library door bursting open. A woman dressed in black strode into the room followed by a harassed Burroughs.

'Your Grace,' she murmured breathlessly, 'I have something of the utmost importance to discuss with you.'

Sebastian was good at remembering faces and voices. He recognised his intruder and frowned. She was the reason he was in this bramblebath. He waved away Burroughs, who hovered behind her. The only way he could evict Mrs Winters—now Lady Smythe-Clyde—would be to have her bodily carried from the room. The hair rising on the nape of his neck told him to listen to her first.

Not until Burroughs closed the door behind himself did Sebastian offer her a seat. He propped one hip on the edge of his desk and looked down at her. 'It is very late to be making a social call, Lady Smythe-Clyde.'

She pushed back the hood of her cape and untied the strings at the throat. The heavy taffeta slipped from her shoulders to billow around her lap and spill down the back of her chair. Her pale blonde curls framed a heart-shaped face with eyes the colour of a fine spring sky. Many poems had been written about the beauty of her cupid's bow mouth. Her evening dress was daringly low, even for a married woman, and showed an almost childlike figure. Sebastian knew the heart of a courtesan beat under the small bosom. But why was she here? He had already refused her overtures.

She smiled endearingly up at him. 'Please, your

Grace, do call me Emily. We shall soon be well acquainted.'

'Shall we?' he murmured, wondering what her game was and knowing it boded no good for him or the girl upstairs. He knew the former Mrs Winters from old. She had been as shocking in her flaunting of conventions as she was as Lady Smythe-Clyde. The rest of their conversation would likely be just as vulgar.

She threw back her head and laughed, a tinkling sound that was her signature. Slowly, her eyes only slightly narrowed, she lowered her head and smiled at him. 'Very well indeed. Do you know where my stepdaughter is?'

Sebastian kept his gaze on her even as the warmth provided by the whisky evaporated. 'Your stepdaughter? Do you have one?'

Her lips parted in a languid smile. 'Really, your Grace, there is no need for games between us.'

Sebastian put both palms on the desk and leaned backward. 'Isn't there? There is nothing between you and I, yet you are the reason your new husband challenged me to a duel.'

She leaned forward, showing the dark valley between her breasts. 'But there could be…'

Sebastian studied her, wondering how far she would go in her pursuit of him. Women flocked to him for his wealth and power. Usually, however, they took 'no' as just that. This woman had been pursuing him for the past month.

In a mildly curious voice, he asked, 'Why are you so persistent? You have an older husband who is titled and reasonably wealthy. Isn't that enough, considering where you started life?'

An angry scowl marred her childish beauty before she smoothed her brow with an index finger. 'My husband is not the Duke of Brabourne, one of the most influential men in the realm.' She paused for effect and flicked her small pink tongue along her bottom lip. 'Nor is he renowned as the best lover in England, a man all women find irresistible—in and out of bed.'

Sebastian's gut tightened. He dipped his head to her in mocking acknowledgement of her statement.

His father had never thought of him as more than a means to pass on the title. His mother had never thought of him at all, her own lovers being legendary and all-consuming.

In an attempt to be more than a title and money, he had taught himself to be a lover. He had made himself into a man women remembered, and if it was by giving them more pleasure than any thought possible, then so be it. They would remember him as more than a wealthy Duke, an object of advancement. They would remember him as a man.

But not this woman. He had not even kissed her,

and she had already caused him more problems than any of his numerous mistresses put together.

He smiled, a cold stretching of his sensual lips. 'Lady Smythe-Clyde, I would never presume to enter a dalliance with a married woman.'

Her own smile was equally frigid. 'You would do whatever you damn well pleased, and we both know it.'

'Ah, the gloves are off,' he murmured.

'As will be more than that,' she countered, 'if you know what is good for your future.'

'Are you threatening me?' he asked, his voice silky.

She smoothed the satin of her skirt, the action drawing attention to the fine lines of her thighs, her gaze never leaving his face. 'Nothing so dramatic. Merely offering not to divulge some information my lady's maid was so obliging as to find out for me.'

He did not need an explanation. Somehow, even with all his efforts to keep Juliet Smythe-Clyde's presence in his house secret, one of the servants had found out and spread the information. Eventually the news would spread to other homes of the *ton*. And quickly.

Whether he agreed to the dalliance being proposed or refused, the result would be the same. Juliet Smythe-Clyde was ruined.

'Just why exactly are you pursuing me?' he wondered. 'There are plenty of other men who would be eager to accept what you offer. And,' he added in an aside, 'I have it on good authority that some of them are very good in bed.'

She rose and sauntered to him. Running her index finger down his shirt, she watched him through thick blonde lashes. 'But none of them are you. You are rich and powerful…and appealing. You can raise me in the eyes of the *ton*. My husband cannot. He is a mere baron, and an old, fat one at that. He has no fire.' Her eyes took on a sultry gleam. 'And I desire you.'

Sebastian's lip curled. 'If you are so quick to cheat on him, then perhaps you should not have married him.'

Her tinkling laugh rang out as she stood on tiptoe and lightly kissed him. 'Do not come the naïve with me. You, of all people, know about women marrying men and then having *cicisbeos*.'

Sebastian stiffened, her words like ice sliding down his spine. Anger immediately followed—an anger so intense it would have melted any amount of ice.

'Out.' He spoke softly, but the menace of his posture clearly conveyed itself. 'Out before I wring your very lovely neck.'

The former Mrs Winters rose abruptly. Her fingers shook as she tied her cape around her shoulders. Still, she met his unyielding gaze without flinching.

'Do not take long to make up your mind, *Brabourne*. I am not a patient woman.'

He watched her sweep from the room, the heavy scent of jasmine lingering. Yes, he knew about women who cheated on their husbands. No matter what the repercussions, he would not be the one to help her cuckold Smythe-Clyde. Dallying with married women was one vice he did not have.

Chapter Four

Juliet woke from a laudanum-induced slumber. Her shoulder throbbed and her eyes felt gummed over. Her mouth was filled with cotton, or so it seemed.

A brace of candles flickered on the mantel, their golden light illuminating a chair and table. The Duke lounged in what she thought of as his favourite piece of furniture, one hand holding a wine glass. She must have made a noise because he turned to look at her.

'I see you are finally awake. Ferguson must have overdone the laudanum last time.'

He rose and moved to the bed. She watched him in fascination. Perhaps it was her illness, but it seemed that he became more intriguing each time she woke. No wonder women flocked to him.

He put a cool hand on her forehead, and she jerked. He gazed quizzically down at her, a small smile curving his sensual lips. He was very aware of his effect on her.

'You are not as warm as earlier. Ferguson's poultice works. A good thing. You are going home tonight.'

'Going home?' she echoed, feeling stupid, but still reacting to his touch.

He nodded. 'There has been a new development and it is best that you leave. I am sending Mrs Burroughs with you. She will keep people from bothering you and provide the perfect alibi.'

'Alibi?' It was the remnants of the drug making her sound so dull.

The cold hauteur she associated with him returned, making his eyes resemble ice. 'Yes, alibi. Ferguson will drive you up to your home this evening and you will alight from your own carriage with Mrs Burroughs. Everyone will be told you had to make an emergency trip to visit your old nanny. Ferguson says she lives close enough that the excuse is plausible.

Juliet nodded, beginning to understand. 'But I cannot return in your nightshirt or Harry's clothes.'

'Do you think we are such poor conspirators?'

'Why don't I have my own maid, then?' she asked archly.

He stared at her for a moment. 'Why indeed? Let me think.' After a pause, he added, 'She was out running an errand for you when word of your old nanny's plight reached you. You did not have time to wait for the servant's return, you were so fearful of what might happen if you delayed.'

'And I paid Mrs Burroughs out of my pin money?'

'What else?' he countered, a devastating smile playing over his lips. 'Don't tell me your Papa keeps you on a short lead, for I shan't believe it. If he did so, you would never have been able to sneak off and meet me for the duel without someone finding out.'

'True,' she muttered. 'Neither Papa nor Emily care much what I do. Harry does, but he is too intrigued by his first visit to London to pay much attention to me. And since I run the household, it is easy to do as I please.'

'Exactly,' he stated.

She shook her head, amazed at his ingenuity and correct reading of her situation, and instantly regretted it. Her ears rang and dizziness made her close her eyes.

'Are you all right?' he asked, a tinge of anxiety in his voice.

She managed a tight smile. 'Yes. I have no intention of staying here longer and causing you further trouble.' She took several deep, slow breaths before opening her eyes. 'Did Hobson manage to get some of my clothes?'

'Yes. Your servants are loyal to foolhardiness,'

he said curtly, disapproval obvious in the stiffness of his shoulders.

Her smile came again, softer. 'They have always been there to help. Mama used to say she would not accomplish half of what she did if not for them. They came with her when she married Papa. Hobson was a footman then, and Ferguson a stable boy.'

'Old family retainers. That explains a lot.'

A soft knock was followed by Mrs Burroughs' appearance. 'Your Grace. Miss.' She billowed into the room, her arms full of clothing. 'Now, you must leave,' she said to Brabourne, 'while I help Miss Juliet dress. I will let you know when to return.'

The Duke made a sardonic bow and left.

Mrs Burroughs helped Juliet sit up with pillows propping her back. From then on everything was agony, and it was only stubbornness that kept Juliet from fainting. She was going home. No longer would she be beholden to the man she had tried to shoot.

Juliet woke to the scents of lavender and lilac. She had to be in her own room because she always kept bowls of the dry flowers and fresh when they were in season. She stretched and winced. Her shoulder hurt.

Everything came back in a rush. The duel, the wound, the Duke. The last thing she remembered was him kissing her hand as he helped her into the carriage. The arrival home and her getting to her room were a blur.

She forced herself to a sitting position and stopped. Her head spun, and it was all she could do not to collapse back on to the pillows. She would have to move more slowly.

After what seemed an eternity the room stopped twirling. She swallowed, her tongue feeling swollen and dry. A little water would be nice. A glance at the bedside table showed a pitcher and glass. Careful not to set off another dizzy spell, she poured the liquid and drank it down. It tasted like ambrosia.

Only now did she notice that she was dressed in her favourite nightrail. She looked around, noting the shades of lilac and lavender in drapes, carpet and bed-covering. Being in her own room provided a sense of comfort and security that she had not realised she was missing until now. It was wonderful.

A knock alerted her instants before the door opened. A short, robust lady with a grey bun and iron-straight eyebrows slipped in, quickly closing the door behind herself. Mrs Burroughs. She held a silver tray from which came the smell of hot chocolate and toast. Juliet stared as the woman set the tray on a table by the fire.

'Thank you, Mrs Burroughs. I feel as weak as a newborn pup.'

'I've just the thing, then, Miss Juliet,' the house-keeper said, a twinkle in her brown eyes. 'I see you are much better, just as Ferguson said you would be. 'Tis a good thing you hired me as your lady's maid for the last several days while you went to visit your old nanny. Bless the lady's heart, being so sick and all that she needed you immediately and left you no time to notify your father. Unfortunately, your note did not arrive till today.'

The Duke had thought of everything.

She crossed to the bed and put a sturdy arm around Juliet's waist and helped her to a chair. Juliet sank like a rock on to the lavender silk cushion of her favourite chair. She was so tired.

'How long will you be staying? It seems that I am not up to snuff yet.'

Mrs Burroughs smiled gently. 'As long as needed. I have already had the devil of a time keeping your own maid out. The only thing that has saved us is the fact that you hired the girl here in London and she has no loyalty to you. Now, take some hot choc-olate and toast. You need plenty of nourishment to regain your strength.' She frowned as Juliet sipped the drink. 'I would give you some laudanum, for I know your shoulder pains you a great deal, but you will need all your wits about you today.'

Juliet sighed. 'So true. Emily will very likely be here at any moment, demanding to know why I took off like I did.'

'Tut, tut, child. We will get through this.'

Juliet nibbled a triangle of toast, her dry mouth

making it difficult to swallow. 'How long exactly was I at Lord Brabourne's? I seem to remember him saying two or three days.'

'Two nights and three days.'

Two nights and three days. Papa. The duel. She turned an anxious gaze to the other woman. 'What about Papa? Did he meet the Duke? Did Brabourne shoot him?'

'They met,' Mrs Burroughs said softly.

'Why was I not told?' Juliet demanded, trying to push herself up and failing.

'There, there. The Duke felt it was better that you not know. He did not want the worry causing a relapse.'

'It must have been while I was drugged with laudanum.'

Mrs Burroughs rearranged the pillow behind Juliet's back. 'It was, but everything is fine now. The Duke's bullet went wide and your Papa shot into the ground. No one was hurt.'

Juliet sagged in relief and a shiver of aftershock shook her. 'Then my foolishness accomplished something.'

'More than you know, child,' Mrs Burroughs murmured, a strange look on her face. 'But you are trembling. Where do you keep your robe?' Mrs Burroughs fetched it and put it around Juliet's shoulders.

Juliet huddled into the warmth of her lilac robe

as another thought erupted. 'He could have shot
Papa, but did not. Why? Is he admitting that he dal-
lied with my stepmother?'

Fierceness toughened Mrs Burroughs's features.
'His Grace saved your Papa a nasty wound. That is
not admitting anything. The Duke would never become involved with a married woman. Never.'

Juliet glanced at the older woman, surprised by
her vehemence. It seemed that Brabourne also com-
manded loyalty. Juliet took a gulp of too-hot chocolate and choked. 'Ahh!'

Mrs Burroughs was instantly solicitous, her ire of
seconds before forgotten. 'Are you all right?' Juliet
nodded and wiped the tears of pain away with one
hand. 'Are you always so impetuous? If so, the two
of you will make quite a pair.'

Juliet put the china cup down on to the saucer
with such force the chocolate sloshed over the
edges. She stared at the woman and wondered if her
hearing had been impaired by her injury.

'Whatever are you talking about?'

'You are stubborn like him, too.'

'Are we still discussing Brabourne?' Juliet asked
with an underlying chill in her voice.

Mrs Burroughs sighed. 'You do not like him.
Well, that is understandable. He does not have a
good reputation, and he goes his own way and the
devil take the hindmost. And he is arrogant.' She
moved to the bed and straightened the cover but,

even with her back to Juliet her words were clear. 'He came into his title young. Much too young. And he had a disappointment that made him bitter and hard. But he's good and honourable at heart.' She sighed again, her ample bosom rising and falling like a tidal wave. 'He just needs a situation to make him act good and honourable.' She turned to face Juliet and pinned her with intense brown eyes. 'You are that situation.'

Juliet's eyes widened, and her head jerked back at the force of the other woman's look and words. 'Me? are you mad?'

'No.' She leaned down to Juliet, her face serious and her voice lowered so that Juliet had to strain to hear. 'We tried to keep your presence in his Grace's home secret. We did everything we could think of, but somehow it leaked out. We made up the story of your whereabouts for your family and we will stick to it, but the rumours of where you really were will be circulating about the *ton* before long.'

Juliet shrank into her robe, thankful for its warmth as a chill of foreboding moved through her body. 'I am ruined.'

Mrs Burroughs nodded, sympathy softening the tightness around her mouth. 'His Grace must marry you, as he will soon realise.'

Juliet stared at nothing, not paying attention to Mrs Burroughs. 'Ruined—and I have not even been presented to the *ton*. I shall never dance at Almack's or have a coming-out ball. All the things I have missed because Papa was busy in the country and then Mama was ill.'

'His Grace will see that you have all those things.'

'Well,' Juliet said, still in her own world, 'I do not need those things.' Her chin notched up and she squared her shoulders. 'They are all fripperies that mean nothing and accomplish nothing. I shall tour the cultural sights here and then return home to Wood Hall where I belong.'

'We shall see. We shall see,' Mrs Burroughs muttered. 'Now, be a good girl and eat up your toast and drink every drop of that hot chocolate. You need everything we can get into you so that you regain your strength.'

Juliet obediently finished her repast. Daintily wiping her mouth, she canted her head to better see the other woman. 'But you can forget this harebrained idea of yours concerning Brabourne. I shall never marry a man of his ilk.'

Mrs Burroughs's lips parted but, before she could speak her mind the door to the room slammed open. The former Mrs Winters, now Lady Smythe-Clyde, stormed inside. Her fair hair curled around her dainty face, and a light white muslin Empire dress flowed around her colt-like limbs. Juliet could understand why her papa had married the woman.

Lady Smythe-Clyde thrust out a clenched fist, a sheet of paper crumpled in her fingers. 'See this?

This is a note to your father. Me. You. From the Duchess of Richmond, saying she is truly sorry, but she rescinds our invitation to her ball.' Her fair face was mottled in anger. 'Because of you. You. Do you hear me?' Her voice rose into a shrill demand.

'I imagine the entire household can hear you, Emily,' Juliet said drily, using the other woman's Christian name. 'You may go,' she added to Mrs Burroughs. 'And thank you.'

The housekeeper hustled out.

'All my work. All my careful planning and it is all coming to naught,' Emily fumed as she paced the floor.

'I know this is a great disappointment to you, after all your plans and hard work to present me to Society.' Juliet managed to keep a tone of sympathy in her voice, even though she knew the other woman had merely used her as a reason for her pursuit of the *ton*.

Emily stopped in her tracks and a curl of contempt marred her otherwise perfect mouth. 'Let us lay off this game-playing, Juliet, for I am prodigiously tired of it. Bringing you out was to be my introduction to Polite Society; now, through your ill-judged stay in the Duke of Brabourne's house, you have put paid to everything I have worked so hard to achieve.'

Juliet suppressed a jolt of shock. How did Emily know? Surely the rumours had not reached here yet?

'How can you say that? I have been with my old nurse.'

Emily's lips curled. 'Save that twaddle for others. I know the truth.'

Juliet eyed the other woman but said nothing, waiting to see what would happen. There were times when she managed not to react. Few, but occasionally.

'Oh, yes.' Emily moved to the fireplace and threw the paper into the flames. 'In fact, it was I who let slip the secret of your whereabouts.'

Juliet gasped, all her careful control slipping. 'You? Why? If I am ruined, then everything you have done to enter Society is in vain.'

A cruel light hardened the other woman's eyes. 'I made the best of a bad situation. Sooner or later someone would have found out. I just speeded up the revelation.'

The words did not make sense, and Juliet wondered if she was still suffering from too much laudanum, as she had at the Duke's house. Or perhaps it was exhaustion. 'I don't understand.'

Emily gave Juliet a contemptuous once-over. 'No, you would not. Miss Prim and Proper. Always doing what is best for Papa, without a care about anything else.'

Juliet was taken aback. She knew the other woman did not like her, and she did not like her stepmother, but the venom was more pronounced than she had expected. Still, the insults fired her already edgy nerves and she spoke hastily. 'Someone has to care for Papa, for it is obvious that you do not.'

A tinkling laugh filled the room. 'I did not marry him to care for him. I married him for position and to be cared for by him.'

Juliet saw red. This woman had married Papa with no regard for anyone else. Not that she had ever doubted it, but…but there had always been a kernel of hope that she was wrong.

'If you wanted position and care, why did you not marry a man like Brabourne instead of merely dallying with one? At least then the rest of us would not be in this mess.'

Emily gave a bark of laughter, as different from her famous trill as black was from white. 'Do you think I did not try?'

Juliet looked in horror at Emily. 'So Papa is nothing to you. Only a means to an end.'

The other woman sniffed. 'All marriages of our class are arrangements. At least your papa does not need an heir. So I am free to go my own way.'

'Which you did with Brabourne,' Juliet said, her anger simmering. The small twinge of discomfort she felt at the thought of Emily in the Duke's arms was squashed.

Emily shrugged. 'For a while.'

'You are selfish. If you had been more discreet,

Papa would not have needed to challenge Brabourne
to a duel, and none of this would have happened.'
Juliet made her hands unclench. It was past. There
was nothing she could do to change the current situation.

'So, the ever-so-dutiful and solicitous daughter
has claws. Well, I never doubted it.' She turned her
back to Juliet. 'If you had been less impetuous, we
would not be in this situation. No one said you had
to take your father's place.'

Juliet struggled to her feet, no longer willing to
look up at the other woman. Dizziness made her
grab the back of the chair, but she remained standing. 'Someone had to protect Papa from your folly.'

Emily sneered. 'And who will protect him from
this unpleasant mess your reckless action has
caused?'

'My reckless action? You are the one who let the
information out, for which reason you still have not
told me.' Her fingers clenched the chair until her
knuckles turned white. She was so tired, but she
could not let Emily leave without finding out what
was going on.

Emily took in Juliet's discomfort. 'It would seem
you have returned too soon. You will need to stay
in bed for some time to come.'

Juliet's chest tightened in anger. 'I will do as I
see fit.'

Emily arched two perfectly cared-for blonde

brows. 'Will you? We shall see what your papa has to say about your…exhaustion.'

Juliet nearly toppled over. For the first time since this argument began she realised that if Emily knew what had really happened then Papa could find out. That would hurt Papa. Something she did not want.

In a tired voice, all the fight drained from her, Juliet asked, 'Why are you doing this?'

Emily glared at her. 'Because if I cannot have Brabourne, and all that he represents in Society, I will see to it that you have him and I benefit directly from your connection to him. When the Duke decides he has to save your reputation and asks you to marry him, I expect you to accept.'

Juliet stiffened her spine, knowing she was nearly ready to collapse. 'You are crazy. He will never ask and I would never accept.'

Emily moved to the door and gave Juliet a last penetrating look. 'Do not be too sure about what either of you will do.'

Juliet stared at the door long after the other woman had left. Insanity. This was the stuff farces were made of. Brabourne would never propose. Never.

And if he did? a tiny voice asked. Juliet sank back into the chair and covered her eyes with a shaking hand. She would resist him, no matter how hard or how much it hurt. There was no other answer when a rake came calling.

* * *

Mrs Burroughs gave him the minimum curtsy required, and Sebastian could tell by the look on her face that she longed to box his ears. If anyone else looked at him the way she did, they would soon regret it. With her he merely sighed.

'Yes, Mrs Burroughs?'

'It has started, your Grace.'

He raised one eyebrow.

Exasperation lowered hers. 'The ostracism of the young lady. Just as I knew it would. Just as you knew it would—if you had let yourself consider it. You must stop it.'

This woman was one of the few people in his life he cared for, and the only woman. But, right now, irritation at her persistence in pushing him about something he did not want to do hardened his jaw. For the first time since becoming an adult he was curt with her.

'I am busy now, Mrs Burroughs, and have no time to discuss this matter. Nor will I ever.' He stood so that he towered above her rotund figure. 'Do I make myself clear?'

She inflated her chest and lifted her ample chin. 'Quite…your Grace.' Without asking permission to leave, she sailed out.

Sebastian watched her until she was gone, then turned to look out through the large window that let the meagre afternoon sunlight into the library. The roses were in full bloom and a few tulips lingered.

The girl was becoming an even bigger problem. Much as he did not want to become involved, he wanted to see her ostracised even less. She had spirit. And she cared about others.

He remembered her reason for dressing as a boy and fighting him. It had all been for her father. Never once had she mentioned or seemed even to consider the repercussions to herself. He admired that trait in anyone, since it was so unusual, but in the girl he found himself more than admiring.

Making a decision, he turned and strode to the door. He went into the hall and beckoned to a nearby footman. 'Fetch Mr Wilson for me. Now.'

'Yes, your Grace.' The young man bowed and hurried off.

Sebastian returned to the library and sprawled out in the leather wingchair that was his favourite. He did not wait long for the knock.

Jeremy Wilson entered the room, his fair blond hair glinting in the light. He was a slight man. The kind that mothers wanted to nurture and women wanted to protect. Men liked him too. Sebastian trusted and depended on him.

'Jeremy, my long-suffering secretary,' Sebastian said, waving him to a seat. 'I have yet another job for you that has nothing to do with my business affairs. And hopefully, after a short while, will have nothing to do with my social life either.'

Jeremy grinned. 'Another woman, your Grace?

Most men would be more than happy to be pursued at all hours and all days. You seek to get rid of them.'

Sebastian returned the smile from habit, not amusement. 'Ah, but then I am not most men. Besides, all women become bores sooner or later.'

A flash of pity filled Jeremy's green eyes, but only for a second. 'What can I do this time, your Grace?'

Sebastian straightened in the chair. 'I want you to find out the engagements of Lord Smythe-Clyde and his family.'

The secretary's eyes widened. The Duke had asked many unusual things of him, but never something like this.

'Yes,' Sebastian said drily, 'the same man who challenged me to a duel over his wife. And you may as well know, since I know you can be trusted and since the entire *ton* will shortly be a-buzz about it, the sick guest we housed for three days was Smythe-Clyde's daughter. She is the one who initially fought me. The later duel with her father was a sham.'

After a pause, Jeremy said, 'Interesting. I would warrant she would not be boring.'

The comment was too close for comfort. Sebastian ignored it. 'Let me know as soon as possible. If I do not receive invitations for the same events, see that I get them.'

Recognising dismissal, Jeremy rose. 'I should have some information by this afternoon. Oh, yes, you are invited to the Duchess of Richmond's ball. It is tonight. I understand that everyone has been asked.'

'Including the Smythe-Clydes?'

'I would assume so,' Jeremy said from the door.

Sebastian rubbed his right eyebrow. 'Her events are always overcrowded and uninteresting, but I suppose I must attend if I intend to put my plan into action.'

Jeremy waited to see if his employer would elaborate. When the Duke rose and turned to look out of the window, Jeremy understood he would learn nothing more.

Sebastian heard the door close. He wondered one last time why he was concerning himself. It had been a long time since he had done something for someone else who was not one of his cronies. It was a strange sensation.

Sebastian put the final crease in his cravat, his valet looking on proudly. 'A perfect Brabourne Soirée,' the servant said reverentially.

Ravensford lounged nearby on the bed, a wicked gleam in his eyes. 'All the ladies will be in awe of your sartorial elegance.'

Sebastian cut him a fulminating glance as his valet helped him into a sleekly tailored blue jacket. A thumb-sized sapphire secured in the cravat was the final touch.

'Where is Perth?' Sebastian asked.

'Carousing in some den of iniquity. He did not tell me which one, so I'm afraid we cannot plan on joining him later.'

'More's the pity,' Sebastian said, attaching a silver fob to his waistcoat. 'he will have more fun than we.'

'Without a doubt,' Ravensford said, rising from the bed and straightening his coat. 'But we are on a mission.'

'Here, my lord,' the valet said, hurrying over to Ravensford. 'Let me brush out the wrinkles and straighten your collar and cravat.'

'No need, Roberts,' Ravensford said, fending of the servant's eager help. 'I don't mind a little mussing. I am a Corinthian, not a dandy.'

Roberts backed away, but could not keep from sighing. 'You could cut such a dashing figure, my lord, if I may be so bold as to say.'

'He already does,' Sebastian said with a mocking grin. 'He is the epitome of raffishness. All the women will swoon at his feet.'

'There is only one kind of woman I want swooning,' Ravensford said, 'and we will not find that kind at this gathering.'

'No,' Sebastian said, opening the door. 'And more's the pity.'

An hour later, they finally entered the foyer of the Duchess of Richmond's town house. Their hostess beamed at them.

'Brabourne. Ravensford. I am so glad you could tear yourself away from your other amusements.'

Each man in turn took her offered hand.

'How could we resist?' Sebastian murmured, kissing her palm.

'Such devilish charm,' she said, smiling as he released her fingers. 'Enjoy yourselves. There are more than enough eligible women, even for the likes of you two.'

'Yes, but are they entertaining?' Sebastian said *sotto voce* as they walked away.

'Probably not,' Ravensford replied, before turning to greet the matchmaking mama of a girl just out of the schoolroom.

'See you later,' Sebastian said with a nod to the woman and a wink to his friend. He thought he heard Ravensford groan, but knew the Earl was too well-mannered to be so rude.

With practised ease and a cool smile, Sebastian circulated through the room. He ignored the speculative glances sent his way. People had been discussing him since he was old enough to realise what they were doing, and probably long before that.

There was no sign of his quarry.

Guests milled around the enormous room, spilling out on to the balconies and into the gardens. An orchestra played a waltz and couples swirled and dipped to the music. Dowagers sat in huddles, discussing anyone and everything. Several men wandered into another room where cards were being played. Everyone was here, including many he did not know. Except the Smythe-Clydes.

Irritation knitted Sebastian's brows together.

He stepped out on to the balcony for some cool air and privacy. This was the opening ball of the Season. Surely Smythe-Clyde and his family would be here if they had been invited. Emily would be.

A schoolgirl giggle wafted up from the walkway below him, and Sebastian took a step back towards the ballroom.

'Have you seen the Duke?' a girl asked.

'Oh, yes,' another girl answered. 'He looks so romantic. And dangerous.'

The first girl giggled again and lowered her voice. 'He is. Have you heard that he had Juliet Smythe-Clyde in his house for three days and three nights? Although they are saying she went to visit her old nanny.' Another giggle.

Her words stopped Sebastian. His fists clenched and he had to resist the urge to jump over the railing and put the chit in her place.

The second girl lowered her voice too. 'Oh, yes. Wouldn't you just love to be his captive?'

The first girl spoke soberly. 'Not if it ruined me as it has her. Mama said she and her family had been invited tonight, but when word of her disgrace got out the Duchess sent a note telling them they were no longer welcome.'

Sebastian had heard enough. If chits barely out of the schoolroom knew of the disaster, then it was all over town. Nor would he stay here and gratify the Duchess of Richmond by dancing with any of her eligible girls.

Never before had he been made so aware of the double standards of his world. Juliet Smythe-Clyde was not welcome while he was courted, even though she was innocent and he was anything but.

He entered the ballroom and scanned it for Ravensford. Catching the Earl's attention, he flicked his eyes towards the door. Ravensford nodded and began making his excuses.

Sebastian located the Duchess of Richmond and made his way to her. As furious as he was with the woman, he would not be so crass as to leave without saying goodbye. He was many things, but no one had ever accused him of neglecting the social niceties. That was for Perth to do.

He gave the Duchess a cool smile. 'Thank you for your hospitality, but Ravensford and I must be on our way.'

She tutted at him. 'Surely it is too early for the gaming hells, Brabourne. Stay awhile and dance with some of the chits who have been fluttering around you.'

He froze her with a look. 'I think not, your Grace. My morals are not up to your exacting standards.'

She blinked while his words sank in. Taking a step back, she returned his glare with one of her own. 'They certainly are not, but you are a Duke, and an eligible one at that. You can be forgiven many faults.'

'As others cannot,' he said softly, a hard edge underlying the words.

Ravensford arrived just then and took in the situation. He put a hand on Sebastian's shoulder and squeezed hard. Smiling at the Duchess, he said, 'We must be on our way. Thank you for your hospitality.'

She smiled warmly at him and gave him her hand to kiss. Ravensford performed his duty with grace and the two men made their escape.

Outside the evening air was like a cool caress after the stifling heat of the ballroom. Instead of entering the coach when it drove up, they opted to walk with the vehicle following behind.

'What was that about?' Ravensford asked, swinging his gold-tipped cane.

Sebastian took a deep breath and wondered why he had lost his temper. Usually there was only one thing that made him see red. A slight to a girl he barely knew was not in the same league. He told Ravensford what had happened.

The Earl whistled low. 'So, it has already begun. But not surprising.'

'Everyone will follow the Duchess's lead.'

'And there is nothing you can do about it. Why should you?'

Sebastian stopped. 'I don't know. But for some benighted reason I feel like helping this girl.'

'Oh-ho,' Ravensford said with a knowing look. 'So that's the way it is.'

'Hardly,' Sebastian said drily. 'I admire the chit; I don't love her. Or even care that much about her. I just don't want her punished for trying to protect her father. Few enough of our acquaintances would do what she did.'

'True. But what can you do about it?' Ravensford started walking again and Sebastian kept pace.

'I can bring her into fashion.'

This time Ravensford stopped. 'I hardly think so. That will only confirm in the old tabbies' minds that the rumour is correct.' He gave Sebastian a piercing look. 'The only way you can make her respectable is to marry her.'

'A little drastic, don't you think?'

'Depends on how badly you want to make her respectable.'

'Not that badly,' Sebastian said, signalling to the coach. 'Take us to Pall Mall.'

Ravensford followed Sebastian into the vehicle. 'I told you we would not be able to locate Perth.'

'But we shall enjoy ourselves trying.' Sebastian lounged back into the leather squabs, determined to put the chit from his mind for the night.

Chapter Five

Juliet scratched absently at her shoulder before catching herself. The wound was healing nicely; she just tired easily.

Right now, she had to plan the next week's menus. Papa's new wife had no interest in running the house and had done nothing while Juliet had been gone. Nor had anything been done during the past two weeks while Juliet had claimed illness and kept to her rooms, giving her wound more time to heal. No matter that the rumour was everywhere, she stuck to the story that she had been to visit her nurse.

Much as she hated it, she owed Emily a thank-you. The other woman had not told Papa the truth, and Papa was so wrapped up in his experiments that he did not know of the rumours.

Her brother Harry strode into the room and slammed the door behind himself, focusing her attention on him. She watched him with a fond, if puzzled look. He paced the morning room of their rented house, his red hair standing up in spikes on his head. A grin tugged at her mouth. Whenever he was agitated he ran his fingers through his hair until it resembled a hedgehog's back.

He stopped abruptly and leaned on the desk so his face was close to hers. 'Is it true?'

Her fingers tightened on the pen she held until her knuckles turned white. The urge to look away from him was strong, but she was made of sterner stuff. Carefully, she laid the pen down and forced her fingers into a relaxed clasp. Until now he had not asked her, and she could not lie to him.

'As far as it goes. Yes.'

He groaned and raked his fingers through his hair. 'Why, Ju?'

She told him about everything: the duel, her reason for going, and what had really happened during her stay. The only thing she left out was Emily's part in the mess. No one else needed to know that. Brabourne would never propose and she would never accept.

She ended with, 'I suppose I should feel shame for being in his house unchaperoned, but I don't. Nothing happened.' Or nothing of consequence, her always truthful conscience added. 'No one was supposed to find out, but somehow a servant suspected and from there it spread.'

He stood up and his mouth twisted. 'Why didn't you come to me? I would have helped.'

She saw the anguish in his eyes and knew he would be a long time forgiving her. She swallowed. 'Because I am the oldest. I am the one Mama entrusted Papa's care to. I had to do it for her.'

'I could have done it and there would have been no scandal.'

She nodded, her hands once more clenched. 'True. But I could not stand to ask you to put your life in jeopardy.'

'But you could risk yours.' Anger spotted his cheeks, making his freckles stand out like patches.

There was no way she could make him understand. She rose and went around the desk and embraced him. He remained stiff in her arms.

'I am sorry, Harry. I am so sorry. But I could not. I just could not ask you to face a man who would have had no qualms about killing you. You mean too much to me.'

He moved away from her. 'Why didn't you let Papa face Brabourne? Papa is the one who made the challenge.'

She sighed and stepped away from him. He was still too upset to want closeness. 'I told you. I had to protect Papa. To take care of him. I promised Mama on her deathbed.'

Harry shook his head, some of the colour leaving his face. 'You cannot always be taking care of him—or everyone else, for that matter. Some day you won't be here, and then what will happen?' At her stricken look, he hurried on. 'Don't look like that, Ju. Some day you will marry and leave. That's only natural. All women do it. Then Papa will have to care for himself.'

A choked laugh escaped her tight throat. 'I will never marry now. Papa's new wife may throw me out, but no man will take me in.'

His face flamed anew as he remembered the original reason he had come to see her. 'Dash it all, Ju. That ain't true. There is George at home. He loves you and will marry you no matter what.'

A sad smile tugged at her lips, and she turned away so he would not see the emotion. 'Dear George. I would never disgrace him by accepting his proposal. Not now.'

'Don't be a goose,' he said roundly. 'This is not the end of the world. All the *ton* may go to Hades. We don't need them.' His voice picked up. 'I have it. Let's go to Vauxhall tonight. We will forget all of this and enjoy ourselves. Just the two of us. There will be fireworks,' he cajoled.

She looked back at him. He had the mischievous, let's-have-fun look that had always lured her into trouble. Gone was the hangdog expression he had entered the room wearing. This was her younger brother, the boy she had also promised to look after and protect. Mama had known Papa was incapable of anything but his hunting and experimenting.

She caught his hand and squeezed it. 'What time should we leave?'

A grin split his face. 'Half past eight.'

On a much happier note, he left to prepare for their night of revelry. Juliet stayed behind and tried to finish the week's menu, but it was hard.

George's face kept coming between her and the paper. Good, kind George, who wanted to marry her. She had turned him down just before coming to London, and he had told her he would wait. She cared a great deal for him, liked him immensely, and had considered accepting him when she returned home. He would care for her and any children they might have for the rest of his life. That was a gift any woman should be glad to have.

Another visage forced its way to her attention. Hard angles and unyielding eyes made her pulse jump. Brabourne. She gave up. The menus could wait.

She rose and headed outside. The house had a small garden with a white iron bench sitting under a large elm tree. It was her favourite spot here in London. Perhaps some time spent there would ease the turmoil that threatened to tear her chest apart.

Life had been so simple before. It should be as uncomplicated now. Somehow it was not.

* * *

Juliet waited for Harry in the hall, dressed in a simple white muslin gown with green ribbons, her hair piled on her head and more green ribbon threaded through its curls. When she heard his tread on the marble floor she turned to him with a smile— and had to suppress a gasp. He was in the same coat she had worn to meet Brabourne. Visions of that horrible night threatened to close her throat.

'You look very fetching,' her brother said.

His unexpected compliment erased her tension. As her younger brother, she did not expect him even to notice her clothes.

'What is the matter, Harry? Do you have a fever?'

He grinned. 'Thought I'd start us out on the right note. Tommy says all girls like to be told they look nice.'

She chuckled. 'Coming the pretty with me? And where is the redoubtable Tommy? I am surprised he is not coming with us.'

He gave her a sheepish grin. 'He is to meet us there. He knows his way around,' he finished in a rush. 'That is why I asked him.'

'I should have known Tommy would not be far from us tonight.' She felt a twinge of disappointment that she and Harry would not be enjoying their adventure alone, but she put it aside. Young men did not like being saddled with sisters. She was fortunate to have been asked at all.

He had the grace to look embarrassed. 'Well, it

was his suggestion. Thought it would show every-one that we can't be cowed.'

'I should have known. He has been on the Town longer than you,' she murmured, leading the way to the carriage.

The ride was long and boring, but when they pulled up and Juliet stepped out, a look of awestruck wonder radiated from her face. 'It is like a fairyland. There must be hundreds and hundreds of lamps.'

'Actually,' a deep voice drawled, 'there are thousands.'

She whirled around. The Duke of Brabourne, in impeccable evening wear, lounged against one of the entry pillars.

'What are you doing here?' she said, before real-ising it was none of her business.

He pushed away from the pillar and moved to-wards her. The delight of seconds before was sup-planted by an edginess that increased with each step closer he took. He made her feel so vulnerable. She angled back and bumped into Harry.

Harry glared at the Duke. 'He is here to cause trouble, no doubt. Why else would one of his rep-utation frequent a pleasure garden?'

Brabourne raked the youth with a frigid stare. 'We meet again, puppy, and your manners are no better.'

Harry's chest puffed up and his eyes narrowed.

Juliet recognised the danger signs and stepped between the two males.

'Enough,' she said, putting a hand on Harry to
stay his forward momentum. 'Surely Vauxhall is big
enough for all of us.'

'London isn't big—'

'Stop it. Now, Harry,' Juliet whispered, 'if you
create a scene, then everyone will think the rumour
confirmed. What then? Have you thought of that?
Will you challenge Brabourne to a duel to defend
my smirched honour? That would only make a bad
situation worse.'

'She is right, puppy,' the Duke said.

She rounded on him. 'And what are you trying to
do? Make matters worse. I am trying to reason with
him and you put your oar into the waters.'

Brabourne smiled, the emotion reaching his eyes.
'A firebrand to go with the hair.'

For long seconds Juliet stood, transfixed by the
change in the Duke's countenance. No longer was
he the cold, sardonic man who had duelled her and
then kept her in his home. This was the man who
had comforted her as she lay racked by fever, the
man she had thought only a figment of her imagination. The realisation was unsettling.

'I'm warning you,' Harry said through gritted
teeth.

'Miss Smythe-Clyde. Harry.' Tommy's light
tenor cut through the animosity. 'Thought I saw you

arrive.' Tommy Montmart rushed over, his gaze darting to the Duke and back to the brother and sister. He stopped between them and Brabourne.

Tommy was a slight youth with sandy hair and hazel eyes. His chin was more prominent than necessary and his nose was not large enough to balance it. While he was not good-looking, he was friendly and helpful. You could not keep from liking him.

'We must be going, your Grace,' Juliet said breathlessly, taking each youth by the arm and propelling them down the first lane they came to.

They had not gone ten steps before Harry shook himself free. 'I can walk by myself.'

She eyed him. 'Then do so. Away from the Duke.'

'She is right, you know, old chum,' Tommy said. 'Won't do to start a fight with Brabourne. He's a prime one with his fists. Cause another scandal too. The only chance you have of weathering this one is to act as though it is all a farce.'

Harry answered with a grunt.

Juliet listened to them, but her focus was on the Duke. Why had he come up to them? Was he trying to ruin her completely?

Even now, the back of her neck tingled as though someone were watching her. Only one person had ever had that effect on her. She wrapped her paisley shawl tighter around her shoulders and forced herself to look at the sights.

Vauxhall was indeed a marvel. An orchestra played while people danced. Snatched pieces of passing conversations mentioned singing to come. Tommy and Harry talked about going to the Cascade first, a spectacle that even she, cloistered in the country, had heard of.

'Miss Smythe-Clyde.' Tommy halted and motioned Juliet to look to the right. 'It is Prinny himself.'

The Prince Regent stood in the middle of a gathering comprising both men and women. Laughter came from the group like music from a flock of gaily feathered birds. They were the élite of English society. Sudden quiet came over them as Brabourne raised his glass to the prince. Everyone toasted and the laughter began anew.

Juliet turned away.

'He comes here all the time,' Tommy said.

'Brabourne?' Juliet said before thinking.

Both Tommy and Harry frowned at her.

'No,' Tommy said. 'The Prince.'

Juliet turned quickly from their probing looks. She was behaving like a schoolgirl.

A bell chimed and Tommy said, 'We must hurry. They are about to unveil the Cascade.'

Catching their excitement, Juliet hurried after the two young men. All about them others did the same. They arrived in time to get a good position.

The curtain was drawn aside to show a landscape

scene illuminated by lights. A miller's house and waterfall were near the front. The 'water', or so it seemed to be to Juliet, flowed into a mill and turned the wheel.

'Papa would love to see this,' she said to Harry. 'I wonder how it is done?'

When he did not answer, she turned and realised he was not beside her. The crowd had separated them. A man, his complexion florid and his waist ample, grinned at her. She looked away, searching for her brother.

She felt a hand on her shoulder and jolted. It was the man.

'Here by yourself?' He leered down at her.

Shivers of apprehension coursed her spine. She yanked away. 'No. My brother is near.'

He moved closer, his gaze taking in her figure. She edged back, bumping into someone else. Instead of being thrilled by the exhibition, she was fast becoming scared. There were so many people, many of whom were becoming rowdy, and she doubted any would provide help. And Harry had disappeared.

The man reached for her again, but Juliet slipped between a group of people and headed back the way she had come. She glanced behind and saw the man trying to follow. Unlike before, when the lights had delighted her and made her think of magic, they now seemed glaring. She turned left down a small lane with no lights. With luck she would be able to hide.

She twisted around another corner and skidded to a halt. A group of young bucks strolled towards her, singing a ribald song. She looked back to see the man. The singing stopped.

'Ah, what have we here?' one of the new arrivals said, moving in front of her.

A second one edged to one side of her. 'A pretty little maid out for a walk.'

The third flanked her. 'An adventurous little maid. And we can provide her with any thrill she seeks in the Lovers' Walk. Can't we, boys?'

'Yes,' they chorused, closing the circle.

Juliet's chest pounded and the roaring in her ears almost drowned out the voices. This was worse than anything. Worse than meeting the Duke. At least that had been honourable. What these men intended to do to her was anything but.

She swallowed hard past the tightness in her throat. 'Let me pass. I am not what you think.' She was thankful her voice did not shake. It was not as strong as she would have liked, but surely it would do.

They laughed.

'I think not,' the first one said, moving close enough to run a finger down her cheek.

She knocked his hand away. 'Do not touch me.'

The other two smirked.

'I don't think she is interested in you, Peter,' the one on her left said. He reached for her.

Juliet jumped away, only to be caught from behind. Two strong arms held her immobile as the others advanced on her. Fear ate at her.

She had forgotten the man who had originally followed her. She twisted her head to look for him, only to see him gone. He must have left when these three arrived. Her jaw was caught in a vice-like grip that forced her to look back.

'Be nice to us,' the one gripping her chin said, 'and we might even pay you.'

He released her and she slapped him. The blow landed full on his cheek. He growled and swung his arm back.

Juliet was incensed beyond reason now. It no longer mattered that her knees shook so badly she was not sure she could stand up on her own. Nor would it do her any good to talk to these louts. She would fight them tooth and nail. As his arm came forward, she stared defiantly at him. His fist was a foot away from her face when she kicked him hard on the shin.

His arm dropped and he howled. The one holding her from behind snickered. Using the surprise her action had gained her, she swung the same leg back and raked her heel down her captor's instep. He gasped and his hold on her relaxed. She twisted away from him and lunged forward, flinching as her injured shoulder made itself known. The third buck caught her around the waist in a breath-snatching grip.

So close. She almost moaned aloud. The looks on the faces of the other two told her louder than words that she would not get another chance to escape. Nor would they treat her lightly now. Instead of drunkards looking for fun, they now looked for revenge.

She gulped.

'I believe you have the wrong lady,' a bored voice drawled.

Brabourne. Juliet sagged in relief. In the heat of the mêlée none of them had noticed his approach.

He came closer and, by the light of the stars and the full moon she could just make out his features. No emotion showed on his face, but there was a tension in the lithe grace of his movements that boded no good for her assailants. By his side he held a stylish black ebony cane, chased with silver that glinted like fire.

The one named Peter said, 'Go on with you. She was walking in here unchaperoned. We know the type of doxy who does that, and we intend to give her exactly what she is searching for.'

Brabourne moved closer. 'I advise you to let her go.'

'You don't scare us,' the one still holding Juliet said. 'We're three to your one. Those are the kind of odds we like.'

'I imagine you do,' Brabourne said with a sneer on his well-formed lips. 'Too bad you don't have intelligence to go with your brawn.'

Juliet had remained quiet because she was astounded at the Duke's appearance. Also, the cowardly part of her hoped he could rescue her or that they would let her go because he demanded it. Everyone else jumped to his bidding.

In one smooth, swift motion, the Duke pulled on his cane, revealing a rapier-thin blade that had been hidden in the outside case of fine black wood. Juliet felt her captor's sharp intake of breath. The three scoundrels had not expected this.

Brabourne's cold smile widened. 'I never go into dark lanes unprepared—no matter where they are. Particularly not here. It's a pity, but Vauxhall has a reputation for riff-raff such as yourselves.' He took a step closer. 'Release her.'

Still they held their ground.

A gleam of anticipation entered the Duke's intense blue eyes. 'It has been a very dreary day. Nothing would give me more pleasure than to spit you. And I would advise you not to make the mistake of thinking I won't.'

Juliet began to tremble anew. The sense of nerves drawn taut was great enough to make her reckless. 'Oh, please, Brabourne, spit them and be done with it.'

His gaze flicked to her and he saluted her with

his blade, an admiring gesture even as his eyes filled with mirth. 'You are as bloodthirsty tonight, my dear, as ever. Does the trait run in your family?'

'Brabourne,' one of the three said. 'The Duke?'

'Yes,' Juliet said. 'And he would as soon kill you as look at you. He has already killed in a duel. He could take care of you and never be penalised.'

Brabourne laughed aloud. 'She is right. The Prince will not even blink an eyelid at my dispatching filth who prey on innocent women.'

With a flick of his wrist, he marked the hand of the man holding Juliet. She was released with a push that sent her towards the Duke. He sidestepped just in time to keep her from being impaled on the point of his sword.

'That was not well done,' Sebastian growled. Before anyone knew what he was about, he moved in and flicked the cheek of the man who had held and then pushed Juliet. 'You will wear that mark for life to remind you of this night and your cowardly folly.'

The man just stood and stared while his fellows fled into the dark. 'I won't forget this.'

Brabourne looked him up and down, contempt clear in his eyes. 'I don't intend you to.'

Juliet held her breath, expecting the man to rush Brabourne. Instead he turned and seemed to melt into the darkness. Juliet, all the strength gone from her body, sank on to the pebble path. Her body shook everywhere and her shoulder throbbed from all the handling she had received.

Brabourne squatted down, still holding his sword at the ready. 'Are you able to walk? We had best get back to the lights.'

She giggled, unable to stop the release of fear. 'I...yes, just a minute.' She took a deep breath.

He stood and reached a hand down for her. She took it and he pulled her up. She stumbled and fell against his chest, fortunate that it was the side where the sword was not. He caught her round the waist and held her up.

'Steady. I cannot hold you and be prepared should they return.'

She nodded, biting her lower lip. 'I am not usually this giddy.'

'I know.' He released her and she managed to remain standing. 'Stay on my left, away from the sword, and start walking. Quickly.'

She did as he directed. Within minutes they were in the lit area again. People mingled around them, a few glancing at the sword. Brabourne quickly sheathed it.

'Come. Something to drink and eat will help restore your spirits.' He took her gently by the elbow and steered her back to the private supper boxes.

Juliet went without thinking of her reputation and how his escort must look to anyone who saw them. She was just grateful to be safe.

'Thank you. You saved me from…' she giggled again '…A fate worse than death.' She could not stop giggling.

He shook his head. 'You did not act like this when I shot you.'

She gasped for breath. 'I know. But then I anticipated the fact that I might be hurt. It never occurred to me that anyone here would accost me and…and threaten my…'

'I understand,' he murmured, his tone almost sympathetic. 'Obviously your brother and his friend failed to prepare you. Vauxhall can be entertaining, perhaps even magical, your first time here, but it is also frequented by scoundrels and thieves. You should not have been left alone,' he ended on a harder note.

She bristled at his implied criticism of Harry. 'It was an accident. We were at the Cascade and there were so many people. The next thing I knew, Harry was gone. It was my fault for not paying better attention.'

'As you wish. But next time hold on to your escort.'

'Brabourne.' A female voice intruded on their argument. 'Brabourne, I have been looking all over for you. Where have you been, you naughty boy?' She was a voluptuous woman with hair so dark it blended in with the night.

A disgusted look passed over his face, quickly

replaced by cool dispassion. 'Ah, Lady Castlerock. What a pleasant surprise. I thought you were still with Prinny.'

'Of course I am. He sent me to find you, saying it is always entertaining when you are around.' She dimpled at him.

He gave her a thin smile. 'May I introduce you to Miss Smythe-Clyde? She has done me the honour of walking the promenade with me.'

Juliet smiled at the other woman.

Shocked recognition widened the other woman's eyes and pinched her mouth. 'I will see you later, Brabourne.' Then, without a word, she turned her back to Juliet and walked away. The cut was direct.

Mortification held Juliet motionless. Fury kept her from crying.

'Mary Castlerock has been rude from the first day I met her, and that was while she was still in the schoolroom,' Brabourne observed. 'She is no better today.'

His words gave Juliet time to pull herself together. The other woman's action was not unexpected. The *ton* had declared Juliet unacceptable and Lady Castlerock was definitely *ton*. It was Juliet's fault for forgetting that she should never have been seen in public—or private—with Brabourne. Still, the woman's reaction had been extreme, and Juliet was determined that she would not succumb like a whipped puppy. But it would do her no good to stay longer in the Duke's company.

She jutted her chin and squared her shoulders, ignoring the ache that radiated from her wound. She dropped the Duke a curtsy, saying, 'Thank you so much for your help. Without you, I would have been sorely hurt. But I am able to find my brother on my own.'

One eyebrow raised, he said, 'Are you going to let her treatment of you change what you intend to do? I never thought it of you.'

Goaded beyond polite manners, she said, 'That is easy for you to say. You are no better than you should be, yet no one snubs you. No one ostracises your family for your actions. Well, your Grace, I have neither your rank nor your fortune to protect me and mine from people like Lady Castlerock.' A lone tear of suppressed hurt slid down her cheek.

The tic at his right eye started. 'Here, take this.'

He thrust his hand at her and she recognised a handkerchief. 'I don't need that.'

'Take it anyway.' He grabbed her hand, pried open her fingers and stuffed the fine linen in her palm.

In a very unladylike way, she blew her nose. The ghost of a smile curved his mouth. She saw it and blushed.

'I am not very good at being dainty.'

'You are very good just the way you are.'

Her blush deepened. 'I shall have this laundered and returned to you.'

'Discreetly, I hope.'

She searched his face to see if he joked. There was a hint of something in his eyes that made her think he might. 'Most discreetly.'

She tucked the material into her reticule which, by some miracle, still hung around her wrist. Her paisley shawl was somewhere back on the dark Lovers' Lane, and she had no intention of searching for it.

Once again he took her arm. 'Shall we try this again?'

She sighed wearily. 'I am not as good at flaunting convention as you. I think it for the best if I try to find Harry on my own.'

'So, this is where you are hiding out, Brabourne.' A booming male voice made Juliet jump.

'Lady Castlerock said she had found you, but that you were occupied.'

A florid, yet handsome man who carried too much weight headed their way. She wondered if the Duke was chased everywhere he went. It certainly seemed that way.

'Sir,' Brabourne said.

Juliet closed her eyes. This was too much. First Lady Castlerock had cut her, and now the Prince Regent would do so. She sank into a hurried and graceless curtsy, head bowed as much to hide her dismay as to pay respect.

'And who is this lovely young morsel?' the Prince asked.

'May I present Miss Smythe-Clyde, sir.'

Juliet stayed down, waiting, hoping the Prince would not snub her.

'Ahh,' he said in a knowing voice. His tone turned devilish. 'I am delighted to meet Miss Smythe-Clyde. Please rise, my dear. I won't bite— at least, not yet.'

Juliet could not believe her ears. The Prince was talking to her—flirting with her? But she had heard he had a weakness for women, preferably ones old enough to be his mother.

She rose. 'Your Highness.'

'I see why your name is linked with hers, my friend. A very rare prettiness and not at all your normal prey.'

Brabourne's face betrayed nothing, but Juliet was finding it easier to read him. The straightness in his shoulders and the grip on his cane told her he was not pleased with the Prince's words.

Fireworks started going off, momentarily catching the Prince's attention. 'I must be leaving you two. You must come to Carlton House next week, Miss Smythe-Clyde. I am having a small dinner party.'

Without waiting for a response, the Prince left to rejoin his group. Juliet gaped at his back.

'I cannot go to Carlton House alone. What would people say?'

'Nothing they aren't already saying,' he said sardonically. 'But you are right. You will need an escort.'

She nervously twisted a curl that had come loose from the knot on her head, very aware of his attention bent on her. He took her hand in his and pulled it from the hair. He gently tucked the strand behind her ear.

'That will have to do,' he murmured, his voice husky. 'I am not a lady's maid.'

She could not make herself break the rapport between them. There was something magical about the way he watched her. She felt light-headed. Giddy. Ready to twirl around.

'Ju! Where in blazes have you been?' Harry said, rushing up to her and grabbing her arm.

The moment was broken and Juliet felt as though a bubble of delight had been punctured. Everything was mundane once more.

Sighing silently, she angled away from Brabourne. 'I have been looking for you, Harry. Somehow we became separated at the Cascade.'

'I know that. You need to be more careful in a place like this. It may be frequented by all the swells, but there is riff-raff, too. Ain't safe for a girl alone.' He puffed like a gamecock protecting a solitary hen.

'I am well acquainted with the hazards here,' she said drily. Out of the corner of her eye, she watched Brabourne. He looked at her, and she knew he caught her understatement.

'You are.' Harry let her go and for the first time noticed the Duke. He glared at Brabourne. 'Has he been bothering you? For I won't have it.'

Juliet cut off an exasperated retort. 'No. He was merely keeping me company until you arrived.'

Brabourne made an abbreviated leg. 'I think, Miss Smythe-Clyde, that we have found your escort to Carlton House.'

She started, for it had never occurred to her that her brother might come. 'But what will the Prince say?'

'I will explain to him.'

Tommy rushed up just as the Duke moved away.

'Thank you again,' Juliet said softly, hoping Brabourne heard her. He looked over his shoulder and she knew he had.

'What is this all about?' Harry demanded.

'Been cosying up to Brabourne?' Tommy said. 'Not good. Not good at all, Miss Smythe-Clyde, if I may be so bold as to say.'

Juliet shook her head, finding that she was shorter on patience than usual. Normally she could let Harry and Tommy ramble on and rant and rave without any bother. Tonight she was suddenly tired. As calmly as possible, she told both young men about the meeting with Prinny and the invitation.

Tommy's eyes popped. 'Invited to dinner with the Prince Regent? That is an honour. You must go. No doubt about it. Can't refuse. Isn't done.'

'Exactly,' Juliet stated firmly. She took Harry's arm and steered him towards the entrance. 'I am tired and would like to go home. I am still not totally recovered.'

'But we have not eaten yet,' Harry complained. 'The ham is famous throughout England.'

'Thin enough to read through,' Tommy added.

Juliet managed to smile at them. 'I know— Harry, you get the coach to take me home. I shall send it back for both of you.'

The two youths gave each other long-suffering looks. Harry said, 'I shall go with you, Ju. Ain't proper for a young lady to go alone.'

She suppressed a tiny smile. They were so like schoolboys. 'No, you shan't, Harry. I am old enough to take care of myself. Why, I am a spinster. No one will think twice about my going by myself—and no one need even know.'

The two boys exchanged another look, relief replacing the former resignation. 'Capital idea,' Harry said.

They chatted on, while Juliet stood silent waiting for the carriage. The last thing she had expected tonight was to meet Brabourne. And to have him rescue her and then introduce her to the Prince—that was the stuff of any young woman's dreams. But it left her uncomfortable. One dinner at Carlton House would not restore her good name. It would only give more people more opportunities to snub her. Also, it would put her near Brabourne, something else she did not need. She was already too susceptible to him for her own good.

She would have to feign illness the night of the dinner. The tightness in her stomach eased as she thought of this excuse. She absolutely could not go.

Chapter Six

'What is the meaning of this?' Emily demanded, storming into Juliet's bedchamber.

Juliet looked up from her lending-library novel to see a cream vellum sheet clenched in her step-mother's fingers. 'Whatever are you talking about?'

'This!' Emily thrust the sheet up to Juliet's face.

Juliet drew back to be able to focus. The Prince of Wales's crest jumped out at her. Reading quickly, she realised this was the invitation to Carlton House. Only Harry and she were invited.

Juliet opened her mouth to speak, but nothing came out. There was nothing she could say.

'How do you know his Royal Highness?' Emily hovered over Juliet.

'Um…' Juliet rose and twisted around the other woman. 'Now that I can breathe again.'

'Don't be smart with me. Answer my question.'

Juliet moved to the fireplace to give herself some

time. Carefully she laid the book on the mantel and
arranged it so that the spine met and ran along the
marble edge.

She turned to face Emily. 'I met him at Vauxhall.
A mutual acquaintance introduced us.' She waved
her hand as though to dismiss the acquaintance. 'The
Prince seemed to like me and asked me to dinner at
Carlton House. I needed a chaperon so he added
Harry.'

Emily glared, her blue eyes flashing. 'A *mutual
acquaintance*? I don't believe it. Nor can Harry
chaperon you. I am the person to do that. I will go
in Harry's place.'

Juliet clamped her mouth shut on words better left
unsaid. Harry would like going to Carlton House for
all of five minutes. Then the social posturing would
make him restless, while the rich foods she had
heard the Prince served would not be to her
brother's liking—Harry was a beefsteak eater.

'You are right, Stepmama. You will make a much
better chaperon. I am sure Harry won't mind.'

The other woman flounced to the door. One hand
on the knob, she said, 'It does not matter what Harry
minds. I am going. If you wish to argue this, you
may do so with your father.'

Juliet flinched. Emily had Papa obedient to her
slightest wish. Everyone in the household knew that,
and no one crossed her because of it.

Thinking of Papa made her want to see him. She

glanced at the small silver mantel clock. It was two in the afternoon. He was probably in the cellar, which he had made into a temporary laboratory for his experiments. Only his new wife's importuning had brought him to London in the first place.

She grabbed a shawl to ward off the damp cold that was always present in the underground room. She did not know how Papa could stay there all day and not catch an inflammation of the lungs, but he did.

Minutes later, she pushed open the heavy oak door and peeked around the corner. 'Papa?'

'Come in, come in,' his distracted voice said.

She slid quietly into the room. Papa was in the middle of something, and he hated to be disturbed when he was concentrating. His work table was littered with papers and scientific instruments. He fiddled with something that looked like a stack of metal plates. An arc of light that Papa said was electricity shot out. He jumped back, a huge grin on his face.

'That is more like it,' he said proudly. Dusting his hands off on a leather apron he wore tied around his ample waist, he looked over at Juliet. 'What brings you here, miss? Come to see my latest work?'

She always found his hobby fascinating, but never understood what he told her. 'Yes, please.'

'Come over here, then.'

His square spectacles perched precariously on the end of his bulbous nose. 'This is a Voltaic pile, the first electrical battery. I am trying to make a smaller and more powerful one.'

She nodded, understanding that much. But when he launched into the scientific jargon and started pulling out all sorts of machines and pieces of metal, she was lost. Still, she continued to nod and say, 'oh, yes.'

After a while, he ran down. Peering at her over his spectacles, he asked, 'What is the real reason you came down?'

'To see you,' she said, meaning every word. 'It has been days since you have come to dinner or been at breakfast.'

He puttered with his instruments in a futile attempt to clean his table. 'I am so close. I hate to take time away even to eat. But, bless her heart, Emily has food sent down to me. I don't know what I ever did without her.' A besotted look eased the line between his grey brows.

Juliet nearly groaned. She was the one who ordered the trays prepared. Emily took advantage of the opportunity and came down with the servant when the food was delivered, thus making it appear to be her idea. Still, seeing Papa's happiness, she did not tell him the truth. It would hurt him to think his new bride did not take care of his comforts.

'Shall I send one of the maids to dust and pick things up?'

His gaze sharpened. 'Absolutely not. She would

misplace everything and break my most important equipment.'

That was his standard answer. Later, when he was out for his daily ride, Juliet would come back and straighten everything. She had done so since she was a small child, and he had never realised. She was very careful to put everything back where he had it, but she managed to dust and pick up any broken pieces.

'While you are here, what's this I hear about your being invited to Carlton House? The Prince runs with a rakish lot and I am not sure I want you moving in that crowd. Brabourne is one of his special cronies.'

He took her by surprise. Normally he did not involve himself in her whereabouts. It was obvious from his question that he was unaware she was already ostracised by most of their peers.

'Everything will be fine, Papa. Stepmama has agreed to chaperon me. Surely you cannot think anything improper will happen with her there to guide me?'

'Ah, yes.' He patted her hand, his thoughts already drifting back to his experiments as his gaze shifted back to the Voltaic pile. 'That will be perfect. I shall have more time to myself for my work.'

Juliet slipped away, Papa having forgotten she was in the room. Sadness at his lack of interest in her flitted through her mind, to be pushed aside.

Papa had always been like this and always would be. She had to accept that he was the one who needed care. Still, a little voice insisted, it would be nice if once in a while he would talk to her about what she was doing.

The night of the Carlton House dinner was upon Juliet before she realised it. She wore a simple pink gown caught under the bust by silver ribbons. A matching cluster of roses and ribbon nestled in her hair. Pearls gleamed around her slender throat and dropped like tears from her earlobes. Long white gloves completed her toilette.

Her maid—Mrs Burroughs having returned to the Duke's house—handed her a silver gauze shawl. It would be no protection from the weather, but it was a charming addition. Juliet smiled her thanks and left to meet Emily in the hall.

Her stepmother was more than half an hour late, time Juliet occupied by fetching a book from the library and reading.

The other woman was ravishing, her child-like figure shown to advantage by a daringly risqué dress of royal blue silk. There was no ornamentation. She needed none because of the multi-strand diamond and sapphire necklace draping her neck. It was worth a sultan's ransom. Matching earrings dripped from her ears. Her wrists were coated in bracelets, each one enough for many families to live on comfortably their entire lives. Even with the lavish jewels, there was an innocence about her that Juliet knew to be false.

'Here you are, Juliet,' Emily said, as though Juliet were the one who had been late. 'We must hurry. I am sure this will be a sad crush.'

Juliet nearly rolled her eyes. The woman was desperate to go, yet acting as though it were a hardship.

They entered the carriage and travelled in silence. Upon arriving, they were ushered into one of the most ornate and cluttered residences in the world. Everywhere were candles and chandeliers. Nooks and crannies held priceless art. Gilt covered anything that did not move. The brilliance was mesmerising.

Juliet had heard many descriptions of Carlton House, but they had not prepared her for the reality. She stopped and blinked.

The footman paused as well, as though he was used to guests being overwhelmed. Emily continued on through the entry and into the drawing room, not bothering to see if Juliet followed.

People continued to arrive, some glancing at Juliet as they walked by. Many ignored her in their haste to reach the activities.

'You must be blasé,' a too familiar voice said softly. Although Prinny will be thrilled with your reaction. He likes nothing more than to know he has impressed someone.'

She turned to him, noting the elegance which did nothing to blunt his masculinity. 'Were you impressed your first time?'

She knew he had not been, but it was conversation, and her tongue was otherwise tied and her mind blank of anything but his presence. Reacting to him on an instinctual level was the worst thing she could do for her own emotional safety. She knew that. It did not matter. He made her pulse jump.

'Ah, but I watched him redesign everything. I knew beforehand what it would look like finished. Familiarity breeds…shall we say, less excitement?'

'Of course.'

'May I escort you in?' He extended his arm.

Her fingers twitched with the need to touch him. She resisted, ignoring her thumping heart. 'Thank you, but I don't think that would be wise.'

'Usually the best way to combat rumour is to flaunt it.'

She shook her head. 'I am not so brave as you.'

His arm dropped, but his gaze stayed on her as though he were searching for something he could not quite find. 'I know better than that.'

'You flatter me,' she managed to utter around the breathlessness his scrutiny created.

'Where is your brother? Since you will not have me, you should stay with him until you have been presented to the Prince and introduced to several people.'

A wry smile curled her lips. 'My stepmother is my chaperon tonight, and she was in too much of a hurry to wait while I gaped.'

His face lost all expression. 'I see. Wait here and I will send someone back for you.'

She bristled. 'I am perfectly able to fend for myself.'

'Yes, you are. But trust me in this. It will be better if someone takes you in. More proper. Less flaunting of convention.' She frowned and he added, 'Or you can reconsider and accept me.'

She accepted defeat as graciously as her competitive nature would allow. 'I will wait here.'

'A pity, but not surprising.' With a slight dip of his head, he sauntered off.

Juliet occupied herself studying each piece of art individually, the footman still hovering nearby.

'There you are, Miss Smythe-Clyde,' a booming voice said.

She turned and instantly sank into a deep curtsy. 'Your Royal Highness.'

'No, no,' he said, reaching a hand down for her. 'I don't stand on such formality. Ask anyone.'

'Such as the Duke of Brabourne?' she asked, accepting his help up.

The Prince Regent beamed at her. 'He did mention that your chaperon had gone on without you because you took too long admiring my handiwork.'

Trust Brabourne to take the truth and twist it into

something infinitely palatable. 'I have never seen anything nearly as impressive, Your Highness.'

He tucked her hand into his arm. 'You should see my pavilion in Brighton. In fact, I insist that you visit me there.'

Things were going much too fast. Juliet felt caught in an undertow of dangerous currents. 'Thank you, Your Highness. You are far too generous.'

'Nothing of the kind.' He patted her hand and led her back the way he had come.

The strains of music reached them long before they entered the room where the orchestra played. The wittiest, most glamourous and hard-living of London Society filled the vast area. Lord Holland, Lord Alvanley, and Lady Jersey to name only a few. Everyone looked their way. Juliet wanted to sink into the floor.

Brabourne sauntered up to them and, in a move unsurpassed for audacity, asked, 'Sir, please be so kind as to introduce me to your companion.'

It took everything Juliet had not to laugh out loud at his boldness. Some of her tension drained away.

'And if I do,' the Prince said, a gleam of mirth in his eyes, 'you must promise not to steal a march on me, Brabourne. For I know your reputation with the fairer sex.'

Brabourne put a hand over his heart and looked pained. 'Sir, you misjudge me.'

'Not you, but you plead so nicely that I find myself weakening.' The prince took Juliet's hand from the crook of his elbow and extended it to the Duke. 'Miss Smythe-Clyde, may I recommend the Duke of Brabourne to you?'

Juliet made a short curtsy. 'Your Grace.'

He bowed over her hand, raising it for his kiss. His eyes held hers as his lips touched her skin. Chills, followed by heat, followed by shivers raced up Juliet's arm.

'Your servant.'

He released her and she snatched her hand back to safety. Her face felt hot with embarrassment at the marked attentions the men paid her. Never had she been the centre of any group of males, and never had she thought in her wildest dreams to be the focus of two of the most sought-after men in England. Some women would have found the experience heady. Juliet found it nerve-racking and wished it over. But she could not leave the Prince's presence without first being dismissed by him, and he and Brabourne were having too much fun bantering for Prinny to remember to release her.

For the first time since she had met Brabourne, he looked as though he were enjoying himself. Despite all the Prince's faults—and Juliet thought they were many—Brabourne seemed to like the man. The *bon mots* flew between them. Some referred to people and places Juliet could not place, but the men knew exactly what each was saying.

The music stopped, and one of the women who had been dancing left her partner. 'Your Highness,' she said, interrupting the talk, 'we have a bet. Maria Sefton says there are one hundred candles in your chandelier. I say there are three. We need you to tell us who has won.'

He laughed in pleasure. 'Lady Jersey, you are always entertaining. But before I come with you I want to present you to my latest guest. Lady Jersey, may I introduce Miss Smythe-Clyde?'

Sally Jersey smiled, albeit a small one. 'How do you do? I have heard much of you.'

The Prince frowned. 'I think the young lady should come to Almack's. Don't you, Lady Jersey?'

She looked at her Prince, then at Brabourne. In a flat tone she said, 'I shall send the vouchers round tomorrow.'

Prinny broke into a smile. 'Very good of you, Sally.'

She ignored Juliet. 'Now, will you come and tell us who wins the bet, Your Highness?'

He caught her hand. 'I am yours to command. Until later, Miss Smythe-Clyde. Brabourne.'

'Your Highness,' Juliet said. At the same time Brabourne said, 'Sir.'

Juliet started to sink into another curtsy, but the Duke's hand under her elbow stopped her. 'Not now,' he said softly. 'He is very informal at these gatherings. You would look gauche. Not at all the thing, and after he has tried so hard to bring you into fashion.'

'Is that what he was doing?'

He angled a questioning look at her. 'What did you think he was doing?'

She shook her head. 'I did not know. I am not used to this kind of attention.'

'We shall have to fill that void,' he said, propelling her towards a mixed group.

Ravensford and Perth were the only two she recognised. Brabourne introduced her to them as though she had never met them. Ravensford welcomed her with a teasing smile. Perth gave her an ironic nod. Everyone else in the circle was coolly civil, their gazes going from her to the Duke. She knew they would talk about this later. Much as Brabourne had tried to maneouvre, it was not working.

One lady asked, 'Are you here alone, Miss Smythe-Clyde?'

The barely disguised disapproval made Juliet raise her head defiantly. 'No, my stepmother is here.'

'Really?' another woman said.

Juliet was beginning to feel like a mouse being toyed with—not a pleasant feeling.

'Here you are, you naughty child,' Lady Smythe-Clyde said, gliding into the group and stopping between Juliet and Brabourne. 'I saw you with the Prince, but then lost you.' She gave the assemblage a brilliant smile.

The two women who had been quizzing Juliet made their excuses. None of the men did.

Juliet watched as her stepmother proceeded to charm the males. Much to her dismay, Brabourne made his adieux shortly. She felt bereft, not a good emotion to have because the Duke had left. Without any trouble, she faded away herself, finding a secluded area and being thankful for it. She did not belong here. Even if her name was on the tongue of every rumourmonger in London, she was still not up to snuff enough for this collection of the *ton's* most rakish and wild habitués.

Several women, lavishly clothed and jewelled, strolled by. Their eyes met Juliet's and then slid past. Words drifted behind them.

'Brabourne is a devil. The nerve of him to bring his unmarried mistress here. It is just not done.'

The second woman sniffed. 'Flaunting, more like. And she nothing out of the ordinary, with that carrot-red hair and all those ugly freckles.'

They were quickly past, but Juliet imagined that their conversation continued. She bit her lip on the pain that flared to anger. The hypocrites. She might be naïve, but she had heard the envy in the women's voices. It was not done for an honourable man to take an unmarried woman as his mistress, but either of them could have filled the position as long as both parties were discreet. And she was not even the Duke's *chère amie*.

Her stomach churned at the unfairness of it. Her feelings felt raw. She would find the Prince and beg his leave to depart before dinner. Food was the last thing she needed if she was to keep from being sick with overwrought emotion.

Sebastian watched Juliet from an alcove. She looked distraught. When she started walking purposefully in the direction where Prinny held court, he began to worry.

'No sense in following her,' Perth's pragmatic voice said.

Sebastian glanced at his friend. The candlelight flickered on the other man's face, shading the side with no scar and highlighting the one with the imperfection. The slash gave Perth a hard edge that was echoed in the man himself.

'Don't be a hypocrite,' Sebastian said. 'If the roles were reversed, you would pursue.'

A slow grin eased some of the tightness from Perth's mouth. 'I would never have got into this mess to begin with. And never with a virgin.'

'Touché,' Sebastian muttered. 'I must have been out of my head ever to let her into my house.'

'You were unwilling to take the chance that she would die and make it necessary for you to flee to the Continent.'

'Oh, yes,' Sebastian muttered ironically. 'Now I remember the story of it. Remind me in future to have all my duelling opponents checked for their sex before I fight them.'

Perth chuckled.

Juliet reached the Prince, who took one of her hands and drew her into the group surrounding him. She flushed, then paled, but stood her ground bravely.

'She's a game one,' Perth said. 'But if I were you I'd leave her alone for the rest of the night. It does neither of you any good for you to seem to pursue her.'

'You are right, as usual,' Sebastian said, his attention not wavering.

'You had best marry her,' Perth said quietly. 'It will solve a lot of problems. You need an heir, and she needs respectability.'

The Duke jerked as though he had been shot. Perth was the third person, after Mrs Burroughs and Ravensford, to say that to him. As with Mrs Burroughs, he could not be cutting. Instead, he drawled, 'Are you ready for Bedlam? I am not in the marriage mart.'

'No, my friend, but there are times when one stumbles into it against one's better judgement. I believe, for you, that this is one of those times.'

Sebastian picked up his quizzing glass and surveyed the room with a bored expression. 'I think not.'

Before Perth could say more, the Duke sauntered

off in the direction of a group preparing to go into dinner. Even though he no longer watched Juliet, he was aware of her still standing beside Prinny. There was something about the chit that tugged at him, but nothing that he could not ignore.

The Prince Regent continued to hold Juliet's fingers even though he had tucked them into the bend of his arm. She was flustered and embarrassed by his continuing attention. Surreptitious and not-so-surreptitious glances followed them as they walked the perimeter of the room. The others who had been with him when she had arrived were gone, seeing that he had no interest except in her.

'Your Highness,' she said, her fingers clutching spasmodically at his elaborate coat, 'if it is possible, I should like to be excused. I…I am not feeling my best.'

'My dear Miss Smythe-Clyde, I am so sorry. Let me have my own physician attend you.'

She gulped, and would have bolted if his hold on her had not been so tight, or so she told herself. 'It is nothing much, Your Highness. Just an irritation of the stomach.'

He tutted and they continued their walk as she tried to persuade him to let her leave. Finally, when they had circled the room once and were back at the door where she had originally entered, he released her enough to bring her fingers to his lips.

'If you are truly sick, I could not be such a beast as to keep you here. But you must promise me to come another time.'

Juliet had never stammered in her life, but she did now. 'I—I...th-thank you, Your H-highness. I should be d-delighted.'

He released her and she sank into a grateful curtsy, forgetting Brabourne's admonition not to.

'Now, none of that,' the Prince said. 'You are not at court.'

She rose, her face blushing fierily. All she wanted was to escape this awful situation. Others might pray to receive this type of attention, but she was severely uncomfortable.

The Prince signalled to a footman while she tried to think of something to say—anything that would ease the discomfort she felt. Nothing came.

The footman bowed to her and indicated she was to precede him. She made her farewells to the Prince, and left with alacrity. It was some time before her coach arrived at the door. When it did, she rushed down the steps and clambered into its safety. Even Ferguson's raised brow failed to elicit any response that might slow down their departure.

If she never went to Carlton House again in her life, it would be too soon.

Sebastian watched Juliet's hasty departure. She would not even blend well into his world. She was a country bumpkin.

A small hand crept between his arm and his side.
'Introduce *me* to the Prince.'

He looked dispassionately down at Lady Smythe-
Clyde. Her jasmine scent engulfed him. He always
sneezed around the jasmine plant and it was all he
could do to keep from doing so now.

'Importuning, as usual?'

Her eyes narrowed and her nails scratched along
his arm before he removed them. 'I saw what you
did for Juliet. Do the same for me and I will do
what I can to scotch the rumour about the two of
you.'

'You should be doing so already. She is your
stepdaughter.'

'And I am already tarred by the same brush that
blackens her. No one was home today when I went
calling. Previous invitations have been rescinded.'

'There you are,' he said. 'You have stated all the
reasons you should be trying to protect her reputation. Whether I introduce you to Prinny should have
nothing to do with your course of action.'

'Ah, but it does.' She looked up at him through
thick blonde lashes, her head barely reaching his
shoulder. 'If he is seen to enjoy my company, then
all those old biddies who have snubbed me will have
to cosy up to me. It is the way of our world.'

He looked down at her, noting the angelic curve

of her brow and the sweet fullness of her lips. Her looks belied the calculating coldness of her heart. His mother had been much like this woman.

A darkness entered his eyes, and Emily edged away from the barely controlled danger that seemed to lurk around him like a shadow. But nothing could still her tongue. 'Otherwise you would not have gone to all the trouble to introduce Juliet to the Prince.'

'Brabourne.' Prinny's voice broke between them. 'Come speak with me.' His attention moved to Emily. 'After you have introduced me to this lovely lady.'

Sebastian did the honours, a sardonic curl to his mouth as he watched Lady Smythe-Clyde simper and the Prince puff up like a peacock. They made a very unusual pair. If one were not the heir apparent, they would be said to be an amusing pair, so different in size. He easily made six of her.

It took long minutes of flirtatious badinage before the Prince remembered his original intent. 'Come, Brabourne, we must talk and have a chat.'

Sebastian bowed his head in acknowledgement. Both took their leave of Lady Smythe-Clyde.

They had barely reached a position of relative privacy when Prinny said, 'You will have to marry the chit. I have done my best to bring her into fashion, and Sally's vouchers for Almack's will help prodigiously, but neither will be enough. We are becoming a prudish lot.' His gaze swept over the gathering.

Sebastian controlled his retort. 'I don't think marriage would be good for either of us, sir.'

Prinny looked at his companion. ''Fraid it will clip your wings? Don't worry. Women don't expect fidelity from a husband, just financial support and social position. She won't care what you do as long as you keep it quiet.'

Sebastian snorted. There was no other acceptable answer other than yes, and he was not going to say that.

Accepting that Sebastian's answer would be yes, Prinny sauntered off. Sebastian turned away. He would not be forced into a situation not of his choosing.

No matter how sorry he felt for the chit.

Chapter Seven

The vouchers for Almack's came the next afternoon. There was no note or anything to indicate who had sent them. If Juliet had not known Lady Jersey was supposed to do so, she would have never found out. The woman had done as her Prince told her, but in a way that made it unmistakable that she did not want to do so. Juliet had heard that Almack's patronesses would not bow to anyone. Perhaps Lady Jersey was currying favour for some private reason.

Juliet shook her head. She was not normally this suspicious. She usually took everyone and everything at face value.

Well, she did not have to go to Almack's. She tossed the vouchers into the wastepaper basket in the morning room. She had household accounts to go over and no time to worry about Almack's or the Prince or Brabourne. Particularly Brabourne.

* * *

Later that evening, as she read in her room, Harry burst in upon her.

'What brings you here this late? I thought you and Tommy were going to Drury Lane to ogle the actresses,' she teased.

'Isn't that just like a sister?' he said, hands on hips, indignation making his hair seem to stand on end. 'I've come to warn you that the fat is in the fire and you act flippantly.'

With a sigh of resignation, Juliet folded and set down her book. Perhaps she would get to read it later. Perhaps not. Harry could be as impulsive as she, and something had aroused him.

'Emily found those Almack's vouchers in the morning room, and she's fit to string you up by the neck until dead and leave your body to rot.'

Juliet snorted in an effort to cover her laugh. This was no laughing matter and Harry would not appreciate her levity. 'You are too colourful, although I am sure it is an apt description.'

'She is in Papa's laboratory right now, screaming and crying like a spoilt child.'

'Which is exactly what she is.' But Juliet knew there would be trouble. She should have burned the vouchers.

The door to Juliet's room crashed open. She was getting very tired of this. With dry resignation, she asked, 'Don't you ever knock? It is quite rude to enter without permission.'

Emily stormed into the room, dragging Papa behind her. His face was crimson and his glasses sat at a precarious angle on his nose. The leather apron he wore while experimenting still rode his ample girth. He looked flustered.

Emily was scarlet from anger, her eyes ice chips. 'What do you mean by throwing these away?' Her voice rose an octave as she waved the vouchers at Juliet. 'These are like gold, you stupid girl.'

Juliet bristled and said the first words that came to her tongue. 'Only to a social toady.'

Shocked silence filled the room.

Papa stepped forward and puffed his chest, a trait he had just before giving an ultimatum. 'Ahem… Juliet, that is no way to talk to your stepmama. She only has your best interests in mind. You will listen to her.'

'You are such a pillar of strength, dearest Oliver,' Emily said, her complexion easing back to its normal English rose. 'I knew you would support me in this.'

Juliet averted her face so Papa would not see her grimace. She saw Harry turn away in disgust. But no matter how sickened she was, she was trapped. She never defied Papa. Never. Mama had raised both her and Harry to do exactly as Papa wished. Things had gone much more smoothly that way. It was a habit Juliet was not sure she could break.

She took a deep breath and spoke as calmly as

possible. 'But I do not wish to go to Almack's. If I had known Stepmama wanted to attend then I would have been glad to give her the vouchers.'

Emily glared at her. 'They are for you and your chaperon. I shall take you next Wednesday.'

Juliet clamped her mouth shut on the defiant words bubbling up inside her. She looked imploringly at Papa, but he stood beside Emily with a complacent smile. In his mind everything was settled.

She looked at Harry. He shrugged and mouthed, What can it hurt?

He was right. She should not have made such a big issue of this. 'Perhaps Harry can go with us, Stepmama.'

His eyes popped, but he stood manfully. 'I shall escort both of you. Unless Papa wants to do the pretty.'

'No, no. I don't wish to take away your fun,' Papa said. Before anyone could pursue that topic, he left the room, muttering that he had been away from his batteries too long as it was.

With him safely gone, Juliet said, 'Are you satisfied now?'

'Immensely,' Emily said. 'This should be a good lesson for both of you on respect—to me.'

Juliet was so furious she could think of nothing scathing to say. With a satisfied smirk, Emily left.

Harry and Juliet looked at each other. Neither one wanted the signal honour of Almack's, but both were going. It did no good knowing that dozens of young ladies would give their fortunes for the opportunity to drink lemonade and dance to country tunes and, if they were lucky, be allowed to waltz.

Juliet did not want to go. It was just another opportunity for the *ton* to snub her. But she was backed into a corner.

At least she did not have to worry about seeing Brabourne there. Rakes of his ilk never went to such dry and boring gatherings.

Wednesday came much too soon, and once more Juliet found herself in the hall, waiting for her stepmother to make an appearance. Harry, never patient, paced along the black and white tiles like a caged animal.

'That will not help,' Juliet said with a smile.

He grimaced. 'It helps me.'

She was tempted to grab his arm and make him stop. 'You are getting on my nerves. At least stop for five minutes.'

He groaned, but complied. 'You look bang up to the nines in that brown stuff.'

She made him a shallow, playful curtsy. 'Thank you, kind sir.'

He flushed. 'I was just trying to practise.'

She grinned. 'Yes. For your information, this gown is made of bronze silk. My hair is threaded with gold ribbon.'

'I am sure I will need that at some time,' he said sarcastically.

'You never can tell.'

'Is the carriage ready?' Emily's demand stopped their banter. 'We don't want to be too late.'

They looked at each other and rolled their eyes. 'Ferguson has been waiting for the last twenty minutes,' Juliet said. 'And you know how he dislikes keeping the horses still. It is not good for them.'

Emily flitted by. 'It is not Ferguson's place to fret. He will do as he is told.'

Juliet's lips tightened, but she told herself not to let Emily ruin the night. Too many hours lay before them for her to let anger fester.

Hobson put a brown velvet cape trimmed in bronze satin around Juliet's shoulders. She smiled at him. He put an ice-blue satin cape around Lady Smythe-Clyde. She ignored him.

Tonight Emily wore a silver gown trimmed in pale blue ribbons. Around her neck hung a single large sapphire. Matching earrings dangled below her jaw, drawing the eye to her slender neck and elegant shoulders.

Juliet looked away, a pang twisting her stomach. The last time she had seen those jewels her mama had been wearing them on the way to a ball at the Squire's. She had thought mama looked beautiful in the magnificent sapphires. It hurt to see that the jewels looked better on Emily.

Deliberately she blanked her mind.

No one said a thing as they made their way through the London streets. Fog was drifting in from the Thames and the few street lamps were golden hazes that illuminated nothing. The clop-clop of hooves on cobbles echoed eerily.

Juliet was glad when they reached their destination.

They entered Almack's with another group, affording them some anonymity. Juliet paused to look around. Nothing was as she had expected. It was just a plain large room with no embellishments, yet this was the most famous room in London. Some of the most advantageous marriages owed their start to the weekly assemblies here. Disappointment was something Juliet had not expected.

As soon as they were in, Emily left them.

'So much for a chaperon,' Harry said. 'Good thing I am with you.'

'She did it at Carlton House, too. But I am glad of it.'

Across the room, the Earl of Perth approached the Countess Lieven. 'Madam,' he said, making her a perfect leg and giving her a wicked smile, 'would it be too much to request that you introduce me to Miss Smythe-Clyde as a waltz partner?'

She turned sharply to him. 'You are always in the

thick of trouble, Perth. Will you start first off to-night?'

'I fear I must, dear lady. The redhead has caught my interest and I would like to know her better.' His black eyes snapped with life.

She sighed. 'You always were an irresistible rogue. Come along.'

They met Juliet and Harry coming off the floor after a country dance.

'Miss Smythe-Clyde?' Countess Lieven asked.

'Yes.'

'I am Countess Lieven, and I would like to introduce the Earl of Perth and recommend him as a waltzing partner.'

Juliet blinked, then quickly dropped a curtsy. 'I would be delighted.'

'I thought so,' Countess Lieven said drily, and left.

'She does not approve of me,' Perth said.

'You are too kind, sir. I am sure my reputation is the cause of her curtness.'

'That too,' he said, surprising her by his bluntness.

Harry interrupted to say, 'I shall wait here, Juliet.'

She nodded and followed the Earl to the floor. He put one arm around her waist and took her left hand with his right. It felt strange to be this close to a man she did not know. He held her lightly and guided her with sureness.

'I am glad Harry and I spent time learning this. Otherwise I should be tripping all over your feet right now.'

Instead of flirting with her, as he had Countess Lieven, he looked down at her solemnly. The flickering candles cast his face into shadow and then in the next twirl shone directly on his scar. Juliet found him disconcerting.

'I wanted to speak with you,' he finally said. 'I believe you are the only female to ever fight a duel in England.'

Her hands went clammy, and she looked away from his intense stare. 'Why are you discussing that here?' she managed to whisper, fearful that someone might hear. That was the last thing she needed for people to find out.

'I never see you at my regular haunts, and since the incident I've been curious about what kind of female would do such a thing.' He spoke as softly as she. Anyone watching them would think they were flirting and did not want to be overheard.

'An impulsive one,' she muttered.

'A troublesome trait,' he said.

'Sometimes,' she answered with a rueful grin.

The dance ended quickly, and before Juliet quite realised it they were taking their leave of one another. She turned to speak with Harry, to tell him how exhilarating the waltz was with someone you did not know, and came face to face with Brabourne.

The breath caught in her throat and her hand went involuntarily to her throat.

'Oh, you startled me.'

'Would you care to dance?'

It was the last thing she expected from him. Shyness overwhelmed her. She would rather dance with anyone but him. No, that was not true. But it should be true. He was trouble. He was dangerous. To her. To all women. He was temptation, and she was unable to resist.

'Yes,' she murmured, dimly aware of Harry fiercely frowning at her. She gave her brother a vacuous smile and allowed Brabourne to lead her to the floor.

He did not hold her any closer than Perth had, yet it seemed as if she was pressed to the length of him. She would swear she could feel the heat of his body and the curve of his chest against hers. She tried to ease away but he held her firmly, his arm burning a swathe across the small of her back. She shuddered.

'Bronze silk is very becoming on you,' he said quietly. 'Few women wear it successfully.'

His voice glided along her nerves, making them tingle. She was so immersed in the physical reaction he evoked that she nearly missed the meaning of his words. When they sank in, they broke his spell on her and she choked back a chuckle.

'You are so accomplished. Poor Harry told me this ''brown stuff'' looked well on me.'

'I am a rake,' he drawled. 'Harry is but a youth fresh to life's adventures.'

'That is one way of putting it,' she muttered.

'A truthful one.'

She cocked her head to one side and studied him. He was as handsome as ever. His black hair was still longer than fashionable, his eyes bluer than blue, his mouth a sensual slash. Yet…his former cool disdain seemed muted. Almost as though he were letting her closer?

'Am I a an object of curiosity, or is there another reason you are looking so intently at me?'

She dropped her gaze and focused on the sapphire in his cravat. It was the exact colour of his eyes. He must have purposely chosen it. 'It is a bad habit of mine. Staring, that is.'

'But endearing, and not nearly so hazardous as your impetuosity.'

She could not believe this was the cynical, cold Brabourne with whom she had duelled. He was flirting with her, exuding all the charm that made him such a successful libertine. He must realised how dazed she was.

'I am not being fair. For me, our dalliance is just another incident in a string of such incidents. It is my attempt to make you smile and look less as if you have been stunned by a knock to the head.'

Cold water could not have distanced her more quickly. 'Of course. I knew that.'

'I am sure you did,' he murmured smoothly, turning her into a dipping swirl.

The dance ended then and he deposited her next to Harry with a perfunctory bow. She watched his broad back disappear into the throng, feeling as though she had lost her bearings.

Harry snapped his fingers under her nose. 'Are you in a trance?'

She blinked and focused on him. 'Brabourne has a powerful presence,' she said, wondering why her hand still throbbed and her back still felt as though he held her. She was not a schoolgirl experiencing her first dance. She definitely belonged in Bedlam.

'No doubt,' Harry said, disgust dripping from his words. 'I can see the effect he has on you, and you had best get hold of yourself. He will only break your heart if you allow him. For that matter, why is he dallying after you? You ain't in his normal style, to say nothing of how you met and the rumours flying about the two of you.'

Juliet chewed her lip. 'I think he is trying to bring me into fashion, against all the efforts of the rest of the *ton* who are trying to ostracise me. I just don't know why he should care.'

The next thing she knew, Ravensford begged her company for a country dance. Her following partner was introduced by an unsmiling Lady Jersey, who had obviously been coerced into it.

'Miss Smythe-Clyde, may I introduce Lord Alastair St Simon?'

Juliet recognised St Simon as the family name for the powerful Duke of Rundell as she curtsied. She had not risen before Lady Jersey sailed away. She murmured her acceptance and wondered why all these men, who were high in the levels of Society, were asking her to dance.

Lord St Simon smiled down at her. He was a tall man with black hair silvered at the temples and warm grey eyes.

'Would you care to dance or stroll around and talk? My wife would like to meet you.'

'Your wife? I don't understand.'

Although she had a sneaking suspicion, it was one she found hard to believe. Brabourne had said he never went out of his way for anyone. Surely he was not responsible for all these introductions? Yet she did not know anyone else who could accomplish this.

He took her hand and tucked it into his arm. 'Brabourne has said nothing to you. That is typical. He has asked the help of all his friends to bring you into respectable fashion.'

'Very kind of him, I am sure.'

'But not what you want.'

She looked up at him. The friendliness in his eyes eased some of her discomfort. 'This is very trying. I know he is doing what he considers best, but all I want is to go home to Wood Hall and leave London and all its disapproval behind.'

'It is hard to weather the ostracism of our peers, but it can be done. My brother Langston's wife was an actress before they married. She has never been totally accepted by the highest sticklers, but she has enough friends and interests that it does not bother her. You can do the same with time.'

'Thank you for the information and concern. I shall keep it in mind.'

'But not use it.'

They stopped near a woman nearly as tall as he. Her hair was the colour of a roaring flame, and her eyes were like slanted marquise-cut turquoises in the oval of her face. She was stunning.

'Liza, this is the lady Brabourne has asked us to befriend. Miss Smythe-Clyde, my wife Lizabeth, Lady Worth in her own right.'

He looked with such pride and love at the woman that for the first time in her life Juliet found herself envious of another female. The two were very much involved in one another. Most marriages among her kind were for convenience. Watching them, she wished she could marry for love. It was something she had thought about upon occasion, but never particularly longed for.   They were amusing and witty. Harry soon joined them and they treated him with a casual acceptance that won Juliet over.

A sudden hush filled the room so that one of

Liza's laughs sounded like a shout. Juliet looked around to see what was happening.

Her heart skipped a beat.

Brabourne was talking to her stepmother. Emily's hand was on his arm, and her smiling face was turned up to his impassive one. How dared Emily? Hadn't she fought Brabourne in a duel because of this behaviour?

She took a step towards them. A hand clamped over her arm and held her like a vice. Frowning, she looked to see who held her.

St Simon said softly, 'Don't. It will only make the situation worse if you intrude.'

She glared at him. 'Worse? How could it be worse?'

Lady St Simon flanked her other side. 'Things such as this are better ignored. If you make it into a large scene, it will become tomorrow's tea-time entertainment. If you do nothing, it might fade away.' She smiled gently. 'Give Brabourne a chance. He was never interested or involved with your stepmother. She is the one doing the chasing.'

Juliet digested this information. They were experienced in the ways of their world. She would do better for all involved to give way. With a sigh she accepted their advice.

Harry grumbled but, when Juliet shook her head at him he half-turned half away from the couple.

Even so, she knew that, like her, he was keeping them in sight.

Sebastian watched Lady Smythe-Clyde with a jaundiced eye. The woman was a bore, not to mention a troublemaker. He removed his arm from her grip.

'What is it you want this time?' he asked coldly.

Her smile widened, showing white, sharp little teeth. She looked like a hungry cat. 'The next waltz.'

'No,' he said bluntly, taking a step away.

Her hand gripped his sleeve again. This time her nails dug in deeply. 'You danced with Juliet; you can dance with me.'

His gut tightened. He did not like having any woman clutch at him as she was doing. He set out to put an end to her machinations. 'Not only are you vulgar, but you are stupid. After your husband challenged me to a duel, the last thing we need to do is dance together. Furthermore, you complain that no one invites you anywhere because of Juliet. Do not anger me, for I am the only reason you are here tonight. I can see that you do not attend again—or anywhere else, for that matter.'

Her eyes glinted maliciously, but she managed to keep her lips in a rictus of a smile. 'How dare you? I shall see that the little hussy suffers for your treatment of me.'

She dropped her hand and walked gracefully away, a sway to her hips that he knew was intentional. It added fuel to the fury she had fanned. He'd be damned if he would allow her to make things worse for Juliet. He had not gone to all this trouble to have that witch ruin it.

He caught himself immediately. What was he thinking? He had done everything he could and more than could be expected. Irritated with himself, he glanced coolly at the object of his thoughts.

Juliet and her brother moved towards the door, obviously planning on leaving. As they approached a group of dowagers the older women looked them up and down with haughty disdain and then turned their backs on the couple.

Cold fury filled Sebastian.

'Easy,' Ravensford said, having come up to Brabourne without the Duke being aware. 'Anything you do now will only make matters worse than they already are.'

'As usual, you speak sense.'

'But it does not make it easier when you feel responsible for the treatment the chit is receiving.'

'I am not responsible for that silly girl's predicament,' he said, more harshly than he had intended. 'I am merely sorry for her. Nothing more.'

'Of course,' Ravensford murmured.

Sebastian looked at him. 'Sarcasm does not enhance your reputation for easy charm.'

'Nor does anger over the treatment of a mere female strengthen your reputation for cool indifference towards that sex.'

'Touché.'

'Let's get out of here before anything else happens,' Ravensford said. 'White's will probably have something interesting going on. If nothing else, we can get something decent to eat and drink.'

'Agreed,' Sebastian said, leading the way. But he did not feel any less furious over the night's happenings; he just hid his emotions as he always had. His father had taught him that lesson.

Sebastian sauntered into White's, his demeanour at odds with the anger coursing through him. He looked around the heavily panelled room, taking in the regulars: Alvanley, Holland, and others. Slowly the relaxed atmosphere sank into him.

'That is much better,' Ravensford said. 'For a while I thought you were going to explode like one of Vauxhall's fireworks.'

'Those old crows and their simpering daughters are more than I can take at times.'

'Stifling,' Ravensford agreed.

The two men moved to a table where whist was being played and port consumed with a determination that was hard to match. One of the players glanced up. A worried look came over his face when he saw Sebastian.

'What's bothering you, Durkin, losing again?' Ravensford asked with a grin.

Durkin shook his head and gulped down the ruby wine in his glass, poured another and gulped that too. 'Nothing so harmless.'

Sebastian gazed down at the man whose sandy hair and blue eyes seemed to glint in the candlelight. The two of them had gone to school together and, while they were not the best of cronies, they still liked each other. Durkin's edginess meant something was not right.

'What do you know that we don't, Durk?' he asked, using their old school name for the other man.

Durkin ran long fingers through his already mussed hair and glanced warily at his partner, who nodded back at him.

'Best tell him now,' Salter said, his brown eyes looking as worried as Durkin's. 'The devil will be in the fat no matter what.'

Sebastian stiffened. There was only one topic that had ever made him lose his temper to the degree that his friends were indicating would happen here. His mother and her infidelities.

'What is it?' he demanded, his voice harsh.

'The betting book. Best look at it.'

Sebastian looked from one to the other and nodded curtly. In two strides he had the infamous book. He flipped it to the last page with writing and read the content. *When will a particular Duke tire of the lovely Miss S-C so that someone else may have a go with her?*

He slammed the book shut. His eyes narrowed to slits of blue fire as he looked slowly around the room. Most of the occupants met his gaze, a few looked away. Without a word he left, Ravensford rushing to keep up with him.

Enraged, Sebastian was glad he had sent his coach home. He needed to walk. The cool summer night air felt good.

'Bad business, that,' Ravensford said, keeping pace.

'It will be a deadly business if I learn who wrote it,' Sebastian vowed.

Ravensford glanced curiously at his friend. 'The chit is nothing to you that you need fight a duel over her honour.'

Sebastian blew out a breath and stopped. He turned to look at the other man. 'Not right now.'

Ravensford quirked one bronze brow but said nothing, waiting patiently.

'I have resisted the inevitable. Prinny ordered me to marry the girl. You even said I should do the honourable, even though it was none of my doing that brought her into my home. I resisted both of you because I don't wish to be leg-shackled. Nor do I care about flaunting Society's petty prejudices.'

He started walking again, his long legs covering distance like a thoroughbred horse racing to the finish line. Ravensford, a smile starting in his eyes, followed.

'But you can't let them vilify her, can you?'

'No.'

The curt word, with all its implications, cut through the night.

'I knew you would do the honourable thing,' Ravensford said.

Sebastian gave his friend a sardonic look. 'You did. Even I did not know I would go against my better interests because of someone else.'

Ravensford shook his head. 'You are too hard on yourself. I know plenty of people you would help at your own cost.'

'But none of them a chit from the country whom I barely know.' Self-derision dripped from each word.

'You know the old saying,' Ravensford said. 'There's a first time for everything. If there weren't we would not have the saying.'

Sebastian snorted and kept walking. What kind of hold did the chit have over him? Yes, he admired her guts and determination. He liked the way she cared for others before herself. He was even attracted to her physically, something he would not have thought. She was not the seasoned widow or courtesan he normally kept. But none of those reasons were enough to marry her.

It must be something else, but he was damned if he knew what.

Chapter Eight

'I don't want to marry Brabourne.' Juliet jumped up from her seat. The dainty yellow-striped silk chair tottered on its back legs before settling back down.

'*You* don't have a choice,' Lady Smythe-Clyde said, venom dripping from every word.

Juliet paced the room. 'Why isn't Papa here to tell me?'

The other woman's tinkling laugh filled the air. 'Don't be absurd. You know he is immersed in his experiments. Count yourself lucky he even bothered to see Brabourne. Particularly after their past.'

Juliet scowled. 'I am surprised Papa did so.'

'Ah, well, you have me to thank for that.' Emily patted her yellow curls and a complacent smile curled her lips. But only momentarily. 'Considering the state your reputation is in, you should be thrilled by this offer.'

'Well, I am not.' Juliet ground to a halt in front of the window. Outside carriages passed and people walked. A nanny and her charges trundled by like a loaded mail coach. 'If you had behaved yourself in the first place, none of this would have happened.'

Emily surged to her feet. 'Don't you dare talk to me like that.'

Juliet swung around. She was well and truly angry. Her reputation had been ruined because of this woman, and now she was to be handed off to the Duke like a piece of furniture. She was beyond calmness.

'I will talk to you any way I please. We were all fine until you came along with your London airs and little-girl looks.' She lifted her chin. 'Besides, Papa needs me.'

Emily stalked up to Juliet, her head reaching Juliet's nose. 'Don't delude yourself. Your papa is happy now, and that is all that matters. As long as he has me he has no need of you.'

Juliet frowned down at her, all the fight gone like a balloon that had been pricked. Every word the other spoke was true. Papa was besotted with her. She could do no wrong. Everything good in his life he attributed to this woman.

A pang of hurt tightened Juliet's chest. Papa had seen Brabourne because this woman insisted, but he could not be bothered to tell Juliet about the proposal of marriage. Her fists clenched and she pushed back the pain. That was just Papa. He was always like this and it had never mattered before. Except that before Mama had always been there to act as a buffer against Papa's indifference.

Mama. She had promised Mama to care for Papa. She could not do that married to the Duke. She looked at Emily. This woman would not care for her father.

A little part of her hurt seeped out. 'You don't even love Papa. You no more consider his needs than you do mine.'

Emily stepped away, having won the battle. 'In my own way I am quite fond of him. And we are married, a very permanent arrangement while both of us live.'

The supercilious tone told Juliet everything. If she left, Papa would be on his own, or very nearly so. Hobson would try, but it would not be the same.

Nor did she want to marry Brabourne. He was arrogant and cold and…and a rake. A rake of the worst sort. He would marry her, bed her and put his child in her, but he would see other women. His kind always did. 'Faithful' was not a word in his vocabulary.

He would treat her worse than Papa, only it would hurt more because he was not absentminded and focused on experiments. Brabourne's indifference would be true indifference, a cold void without emotion.

'I would rather marry a slug than the Duke.' She stalked past Emily and slammed the door behind herself. Emily's laughter tagged behind Juliet.

A good long walk in the park was what she needed. Since coming to London she did not get enough exercise. Sometimes her emotions built up to exploding point and she wanted to destroy something, anything. This had seldom happened to her in the country.

She called for her pelisse and set off towards Hyde Park. What if she was without a maid or chaperon? People already thought the worst of her; that was why Brabourne had offered. He was allowed every indiscretion imaginable. She was allowed none. Her blood boiled at the unfairness of it and what it had done to her.

When Ferguson pulled the carriage around to the front, she ignored him and continued marching down the walk. He fell in some distance behind and patiently followed.

Sebastian guided his big black gelding around a group of walkers. Ravensford rode beside him on a spirited chestnut mare. They were making the daily pilgrimage around Hyde Park, the Serpentine glinting dully in the summer sunshine.

'So you did it,' Ravensford said when they were safely past listening ears.

Sebastian grunted. 'I could not very well *not* after last night.'

Ravensford shook his head. 'Bad business, that. Sally Jersey gave her the vouchers, we all danced with her, and still some of the pinch-faced prudes cut her. And the bet.'

'When she is the Duchess of Brabourne they will all grovel at her feet. They grovelled at my mother's no matter what she did.'

Ravensford looked over at his friend's tight face. The bitterness in Sebastian's tone was unsettling. 'That was a while ago, and things have changed in the last fifteen to twenty years. If those old biddies defied Prinny, they won't think twice about doing so to you.'

'Perhaps. Perhaps not.' He turned ice-hard blue eyes to his friend. 'I protect what is mine.'

Ravensford looked away, uncertain whether to groan or laugh. 'It is time for me to return home. I have a meeting with Gentleman Jackson that I don't want to miss. Last time I was late he took someone else and made me rebook my appointment.'

Sebastian calmed down somewhat and nearly smiled. 'He is an impudent man for all that he was born a nobody.'

'He is a talented man who knows his own worth.' Ravensford slanted Brabourne a sardonic glance. 'Much like someone else I know.'

Sebastian laughed. 'Yes, but some of us deserve our sense of importance.'

Chuckling lightly, they exited the gate and headed for home. Minutes later, Sebastian saw Juliet storming down the street—alone. No maid or chaperon tailed her, as was proper. She was the most irritating and independent woman it had ever been his misfortune to meet. And he was going to marry her. He shook his head, stopped his horse, and dismounted.

'What are you doing here alone?' he demanded.

She jerked to a halt and stared defiantly at him. 'That is none of your concern. Besides, Ferguson is with me.'

He glanced at the man who had stopped the carriage and stayed put, his attention focused on the two of them. 'He is not a chaperon. Not here,' he added for good measure.

She flushed, and he knew she was remembering her time in his home, in one of his beds. 'He is sufficient. Besides, my reputation is already beyond repair—what is a little more to gossip about?'

'You are the most infuriating woman,' he said coldly. 'I am doing everything I can, and you are undoing it as fast as I try.'

She tossed her head, her magnificent red hair flaring out in an arch of curls under the brim of her chip-straw hat. 'You have gone too far this time, Brabourne. I will not marry you. That is why I am out like this, trying to burn off some of my anger at your audacity in approaching my father. After everything that has happened, I would have thought you would be too embarrassed to even talk to him, let alone ask for my hand.'

Sebastian's lip curled, but he was not amused. 'I am never embarrassed. That is something you will learn with time. As to approaching your father, I had no choice. Something has to be done. Marrying me is the only way to restore your good name. No one, and I mean no one, would dare snub the Duchess of Brabourne.'

'Really?' she said. 'You think you are that influential and powerful?'

'I know I am,' he said quietly. 'I watched my mother flaunt every convention and still be accepted by all.'

He knew from the surprise on her face that some of his bitterness must have slipped out. He did not care. Sooner or later she would hear all the sordid details. Someone would make sure of that.

'Well, that is interesting, but I don't intend to follow in your mother's footsteps.' She swept the skirt of her periwinkle gown aside. 'If you will excuse me, I find I am tired of walking.'

Sebastian watched her stalk regally to her carriage, head up, shoulders straight. He did not mount his horse until she was safely ensconced. And then he waited with Ravensford until her vehicle drove off.

'She will be a handful,' Ravensford said, a glint of appreciation in his hazel eyes.

Sebastian watched him speculatively. 'Perhaps you should marry her.'

Ravensford laughed. 'Not me. My name ain't enough to protect her. Remember? Only you can do that.'

Sebastian snorted, but took the teasing easily. What bothered him was the tiny twist in his gut when he'd suggested that Ravensford marry her. He must be getting ill or be hungry.

'Let's go back to my house. I am sure Mrs Burroughs can find us a beefsteak and ale.'

'You set such an elegant table,' Ravensford said as they set off. 'My French chef is still at Brabourne Abbey. He will be up here in time for my wedding.'

Together they set off, Sebastian putting from his mind any pang of loss connected with Juliet Smythe-Clyde. They would be married in four weeks. Time enough to ponder what to do with her.

Juliet slammed down *The Gazette*. Brabourne had posted the announcement of their marriage. How dared he? She had told him she would not marry him and she meant it. This was one instance when she would defy Papa. This was her future happiness at stake. And Papa's, although he did not realise it.

She surged to her feet and stomped to the wardrobe. She was not going to sit idly by while everything went from bad to worse. She dragged out a black cape, swung it around her shoulders and pulled the hood up to completely cover her hair.

Brabourne needed a come-uppance and she was going to give it to him.

Minutes later she was in the stable, ordering a boy to wake Ferguson. When she and the coachman were alone, she said, 'I need to go to Brabourne's house.'

He rolled his eyes. 'Lass, have ye got maggots in yer head? We are still reelin' from yer last visit.'

She tapped her foot. 'This is of vital importance. Either you can drive me in the carriage and put down a street away so no one will see the crest, or I will hire a hackney. But I am going.'

He groaned, took off his hat and wiped his brow. ''Twould be best if we both took the hackney. I will wait in the kitchen, or wherever Mrs Burroughs can hide me.'

'You are making this complicated.'

'I am trying to protect ye from yerself, lass. You're overly rash at times.'

'This is the only way. I have to stop this preposterous marriage now. I cannot wait until I happen to stumble on Brabourne at some function. It would never happen. I am not invited anywhere.'

'Aye, he will no' be makin' ye a good husband. He is too high in the instep for the likes of you.'

'Exactly. Among other things.' At last he was beginning to understand her desperation.

'A gently reared lass like yerself should no' be
matched to a rake.'

'That is what I think.'

Even though her voice was firm and brisk, a small
part of her—a very small part of her—sighed. There
was something about Brabourne that drew her; it had
started the instant she had seen him dismount from
his horse at the duelling field. Whatever it was had
grown stronger each time she saw him. If she were
honest, it had peaked at Almack's, when she'd realised all the trouble he was going to in order to give
her back her good name. His not dancing with Emily
had solidified it.

She turned away from Ferguson's penetrating
gaze so he would not see the distress she knew
showed on her face. Over her shoulder she said, 'If
you are coming, let us go now.'

Almost an hour later Ferguson was hidden in Mrs
Burroughs's private sitting room and Juliet had been
smuggled into the library. She hoped no one had
seen them. If word got out about this visit not even
marriage to Brabourne would make her respectable
in the eyes of the *ton*.

Her teeth chattered in the cold room, and she
wondered irritably if the Duke was even coming
home. It was nearly midnight. She was rarely out

this late, even though she understood that in London it was fashionable to be out much later.

Impatience ate at her. She started prowling the room, taking out a book here, another there. Brabourne had a very well-stocked library. Her irritation peaked and she decided, in a fit of uncharitable spite, that he did not spend time reading. He was not at all the type she would consider bookish.

She found a copy of Byron's *The Bride of Abydos*, and a smile of pure delight lit her face. She had always wanted to read this book, but first Mama and then later Papa, when he accidentally caught her with it in one of his rare appearances in the sitting room, had forbade her. It was not as famous as *Childe Harold*, but she did not care.

She moved a branch of candles to a small pie table set beside a large, comfortable-looking leather chair. With a sigh of satisfaction, she sank into the cushions and tucked her feet up under her. In minutes she was lost.

The mantel clock chimed four.

Juliet set the book on her lap and yawned. She was so tired. She would close her eyes for a few minutes. She hoped Ferguson was doing the same. He had to be up early.

Sebastian arrived home close to five in the morning, his mood better than when he'd left. He had won at whist, drunk three bottles of excellent port, and enjoyed the company. He could not remember when he had last spent a more enjoyable evening. It had to be some time before that *chit* had come to town.

He let himself in with the key he always kept on his watch chain. There was nothing he disliked more than coming home half-foxed and having servants fuss about him. Even his valet should be in bed.

He turned around from securing the door and nearly walked into Burroughs. 'What the...?'

'Begging your pardon, your Grace, but there is a young lady in the library.' The always-impeccable butler looked flustered. His gaze darted to and fro, as though he was afraid of being overheard.

'Tell her to go home. Or, better yet, kick her out.' Sebastian was in no mood for games and frolic.

Burroughs stepped closer and said in an undertone, 'It is Miss Smythe-Clyde, your Grace. I told her she should not be here, and definitely could not wait for you to return.' He sniffed and looked affronted. 'But she said she would march boldly in if I did not help her sneak in. I could not let her do that. Not when she will soon be your Duchess.' He pulled himself up. '*And* her coachman is in Mrs Burroughs's sitting room.'

Sebastian's mouth thinned. 'Thank you, Burroughs.' He handed over his beaver hat and cane. 'You have gone far beyond the call of your duties.'

His greatcoat came off. 'I shall handle this now. See that Ferguson is prepared to leave.'

'Yes, your Grace,' Burroughs said, relief the predominant emotion in his voice. 'Gladly.'

With a militant click of his heels on the polished parquet floor, Sebastian went to the library. He would make short shrift of this idiotic situation. The tic by his eye started. No woman should be in a single man's house unchaperoned, and a coachman did not count. She knew that, and yet here she was.

He did not see her immediately. The room was cold and the only light came from a brace of candles near the fireplace. Closer inspection showed a figure in his favourite chair. He moved closer.

A book lay on the carpeted floor. He picked it up and a slight smile eased the harshness of his face. *The Bride of Abydos.* Interesting reading. He laid it on the table.

She lay curled into the embracing cushions of the chair, her legs tucked under her so that the toes of her half-boots peeked out from the folds of her dress. Crimson lashes swept like fire across her cheeks. She looked young and innocent. And foolish, he thought, his anger at her actions resurfacing in a rush.

He gripped her shoulders and shook her more gently than he wanted. Her eyes popped open and she stared at him. He watched confusion play in their green depths, followed by memory and then by an emotion he had seen in many women's eyes. Desire.

Her reaction took him aback. It also excited him. Still holding her, he hauled her to her feet. 'What in blazes are you still doing here?'

Her face coloured, then paled, accentuating the freckles marching across the bridge of her nose. She pushed against his chest. 'Let me go and I will tell you.'

'Tell me and then maybe I will let you go.' It was a provoking statement, but he was in the mood to nettle her and more.

Her palms flattened against him, their shape penetrating the several layers of his coat and shirt. The urge to teach her a lesson she would not soon forget entangled with the need to feel her lips on his.

'I came to tell you I will not marry you.' The words left her in a rush. Her bosom moved up and down in feathery motions as she watched for his reaction.

A hardness entered him. 'Of course you will marry me. The statement was in yesterday's *Gazette*. Not to mention that as far as the sticklers of Society are concerned you are ruined—by me. I don't usually sacrifice myself for others, but unfortunately for me I still have enough honour left to know I must marry you.'

Her eyes widened at his cruel words. 'Don't do me any favours, your Grace,' she said, her voice dripping loathing. 'I am more than capable of living without your powerful name.'

'Are you? We shall see,' he muttered, fed up with this game of words they played. He wanted to play another game with her.

His eyes holding hers, he pulled her tight. Her fingers flexed against his coat as she tried to keep distance between their bodies. Desire coiled in him, waiting to escape in a rush of pleasure and satisfaction. Not since his first time with a woman had he felt a reaction this intense.

She licked her lips and he groaned in anticipation. But she was inexperienced, so he needed to go gently with her. Taking a deep breath, to ease some of the tension holding him tight, he lowered his head.

Softly he touched his lips to hers. She clenched her mouth and stiffened like an iron poker. Her forearms pressed against his ribs as she tried to get loose. He wanted them around his waist, pressing him close, as close as two people could be. He shuddered from the control needed to keep from lowering her to the floor and throwing caution and propriety out of the window.

'I am only going to kiss you,' he whispered against her mouth, meaning every word. 'It is acceptable for an engaged couple.'

She gasped and drew her head back. 'We are not engaged.'

His smile was feral. He traced a string of kisses from her earlobe to the top of her shoulder. She jerked against him. He pulled far enough away to see the shock on her face. Her mouth was a round O. He cradled the back of her head with one hand and, with an alacrity he refused to analyse, kissed her.

His lips moved against hers and his tongue teased her into letting it in. Tentatively she opened for him and he slipped inside her waiting warmth. Her entire body responded. He had to deepen their joining. He had to give her the unsettling pleasure she was giving him.

'Relax,' he murmured. 'I won't hurt you.'

She renewed her efforts to escape. He sighed and released her. She skittered away. He was too experienced with women to press her further. She wanted him, but was scared. He watched her through narrowed eyes. She was flushed, her lips plump and red, her chest pounding. Her hands fluttered to her neck.

'You are drunk,' she finally said after her breathing slowed. 'I could…' She edged further away from him. 'I could taste it.'

His dangerous smile returned as he narrowed the distance between them. 'No, merely enjoying myself.'

Disbelief radiated from her. She moved until the back of her knees hit the chair. 'I must go. I have accomplished what I set out to do. I will send a retraction to the paper.'

Fury hit him. He grabbed her arm and dragged her near. 'You are the most stubborn woman. What must I do to make you understand that we are marrying? Seduce you here and now?'

Fright followed immediately by innocent speculation deepened her eyes, only to end with determination. She twisted. 'I won't send anything to the paper if you release me.'

He did and stepped away. 'Bargaining already? I will meet you halfway this time. But don't try my good intentions too far.'

She nodded and warily skirted around him towards the door. 'I must get Ferguson and be gone.'

He picked up the book and held it out to her. 'Don't forget this.'

She looked longingly at it. 'I cannot take it. Papa says it is too *risqué* for me to read.'

He laughed. 'Then you shall finish it after we are wed.'

Instead of arguing with him, she fled.

Sebastian stood for long moments after she left. Her nearness and her reaction to him had left him too aroused for sleep. He might not want this marriage emotionally, but his body wanted it. Badly.

The hackney coach ride home was much too long with Ferguson sitting across from her frowning. If possible, he was even more disapproving than when he had agreed to accompany her.

'Don't say a word,' she ordered him. 'Your attitude says it all.'

He grunted and folded his arms across his chest.

She looked away, watching the London streets drift by. Soon it would be light. They had to reach home before then. So far no one had seen her—she needed to keep it that way.

Strange sensations flooded her body, making her feel heavy and lethargic. Her mouth tingled and she reached up to touch it lightly with a finger. It did not feel any different. Her neck felt branded by his kisses. She wondered if a scarlet line trailed from her earlobe to the base of her neck. She would not be surprised. She dropped her hand.

She was lucky he had stopped. She should be glad. Somehow she felt empty, not fortunate. He had opened a whole new experience to her, and for a fleeting moment, as his lips had touched her, she had wanted to explore what he offered. She had wanted it so badly that it frightened her, this power he had over her senses.

She could never marry him. He would seduce her body and then her mind. Before long she would love him—and it would break her heart, for he would never love her.

Chapter Nine

Juliet stepped into the hall, her wet cape dripping on the black and white tiles. Her arms overflowed with roses she had just cut from the garden behind the house. Their smell filled the room.

'Miss Juliet,' Hobson said, 'you have a visitor in the morning room.'

There was an edge of excitement in his normally non-committal voice. What was going on? 'It isn't Brabourne, is it? she demanded. 'For I will not see him.'

'No,' Hobson said, taking the mass of flowers, 'you have always liked this visitor.'

Curious, she started off without removing her cape. Hobson made it sound as though someone from home was there. She hurried into the room. A man with a familiar stocky figure and brown hair stood looking out of the window.

'George,' she said, breaking into a run. 'What are

you doing here? It does not matter,' she said before he could answer, 'I am so glad to see you.'

He had turned at the first sound of her voice and held his hands out to her. She took them and he squeezed.

'I came as soon as I heard, Ju.'

She saw the anxiety and hurt in his brown eyes and knew immediately what he referred to. 'It is not my choice. I have told both Papa and the Duke that I will not marry.'

Confusion knit his sandy brows. 'Then why was the announcement in the paper?'

She made a very unladylike snort and pulled her fingers from his still-tight hold. 'Because Brabourne is stubborn and arrogant and high in the instep and anything else you can think of that is derogatory.'

George's eyes widened. 'That bad, and your father is still making you marry him? That does not sound like Lord Smythe-Clyde. He is usually too engrossed in his experiments to force you to do anything, let alone something you so definitely dislike.'

'I know,' she said, wringing her hands. 'It is his new bride. She wants to be related to Brabourne to further her standing in Society. She is forcing Papa to force me.'

'What about Brabourne?' George asked, obviously confused.

'Him?' For some reason he feels he must marry me and protect me from the *ton's* disapproval.' She shrugged. 'Silly, but there it is. Once the announcement was in the paper, his pride came into play. No one refuses the great and powerful Duke of Brabourne, whether he really wants to marry one or not.'

'I am more in the dark than ever,' George said. 'Perhaps we could sit down and have a bit to eat and drink?'

'Oh, dear, I am so sorry. Of course. I was so excited to see a familiar and friendly face that I have forgotten my manners.' She moved to the pull near the fireplace and had just gripped it when the door opened and the butler entered, bearing a loaded tray. 'Hobson, you have the manners I lack. What would I do without you?'

The butler said nothing, but he straightened up at the praise. Setting the tray down, he asked, 'Will there be anything else, miss?'

'No, thank you. You have provided generous proportions of everything we may need.'

He bowed. 'I know from the past how Mr Thomas likes his food and drink.'

George beamed as he took in all the refreshment. 'That you do, Hobson.'

The butler left the room with a very satisfied air about him. Juliet sat in a gold embroidered chair across from George and began serving. She asked no questions about his preferences because she knew them all. They had practically grown up together. He was like a brother to her, which was why she had been unable to accept his marriage proposal. Unlike Brabourne, George had been sad, but had also accepted her decision.

'I owe Hobson more than I can ever say,' Juliet murmured.

'How's that?' George said around a mouthful of ham.

She told her old friend everything, omitting nothing that had happened since she arrived in London except Brabourne's mind-numbing and body-electrifying kiss. That was still too fresh and too raw and much too personal.

George chewed a mouthful of biscuit and washed it down with well-sugared tea. 'You have been busy. No wonder the Duke offered for you. It is the only honourable thing he could do.'

She nearly choked on her tea and ended up coughing until tears ran from her eyes. 'How can you say such a thing?'

He took another portion of ham and mixed it with potato. 'Because it is the truth.'

She set her cup down and crossed her arms. 'I don't wish to marry him. I won't.'

He looked up from his plate, hope sparking in his eyes. 'Then marry me. I have asked before and I still mean it.'

She leaned forward and put her hand on his arm.

'Thank you, George. You are the best friend a person could have.'

He patted her and sighed. 'I suppose that means no.'

'I love you like a brother, not a husband. It would not be fair to you.'

For the first time since his father had refused to buy him an exorbitantly expensive mare Juliet saw anger in his eyes, his most expressive feature. He was normally quite placid.

'How do you think I feel, knowing that another man will be your husband? I would rather you wed me and love me like a brother than that you go to another man. I will wait for you to learn to love me as a wife should love her husband. Will Brabourne? From what I have heard of him, I doubt it.'

His bold talk made her blush. 'Would you really rather wed me, knowing you would not be a husband in truth for some time?'

'Yes.'

His simple answer moved her more than any protestation ever could. She began to think it might be the best solution.

'What…?' She paused and took a calming breath. 'What if I never love you that way?'

Some of the hope left his eyes. 'It would still be better than having you marry someone else.'

'Oh, George, I don't want to take the chance of hurting you.'

He sat straighter. 'Then respect me enough to let me be the judge of what will hurt me. I've always known you don't love me as I love you, but I have never met another woman I am as comfortable with as I am with you. That means a great deal to me.' He gave her a lopsided grin. 'You know how I don't like to stir myself.'

'All too well,' she answered, grinning back at him.

'I won't mind how much time you spend with your father.' The look on his face told her he knew exactly what he was offering. 'And you won't have to marry Brabourne. Even he won't dare make you a widow or a bigamist.'

Uncertainty flickered through her mind and she turned away so George would not see her expression. Much as she rebelled against marrying the Duke, much as she told herself she did not want to wed him, there was still that tiny part of her that found him exciting and dangerous. That same part acknowledged that there were times when he could be kind. Chagrin at her weakness tightened her hands into fists.

Without further thought, without allowing herself to feel, she said, 'I will.'

'What?' George dropped the biscuit he was eating. It hit the carpet and spilt.

Juliet nearly smiled. 'I will marry you. The sooner the better.'

Stunned was the only way to describe George. For a second, Juliet wondered if he really wanted to marry her. Perhaps he had proposed because he felt safe doing it, knowing she would not accept. Only she had.

'Ah. Good,' he said, bending over to pick up the crumbs. When he sat back up, his round face was red.

'I will make all the arrangements,' she said.

Relief flooded his countenance. 'Very good of you. We can take my carriage.'

'I will see to food and clothing. We must start immediately, before anyone knows you are here.'

'Oh, yes, yes,' he said, gulping down the remains of his tea. 'Where are we going?'

She stopped in mid-stride and turned back to him. He looked genuinely puzzled. She shook her head. Brabourne would know exactly where they were going and he would take care of all the arrangements too. No, she scolded herself. George is not the Duke. That is why I am marrying him.

'We are going to Gretna Green, just over the Scottish border.'

'I know where it is,' he said defensively. 'I just thought that you meant to procure a special licence so we could be married here in England.'

'George,' she said patiently, wondering if she was really doing the right thing and immediately telling herself she had no other choice, 'I am a woman. I cannot get a special licence. If we were going to do that, you would have to do it. Besides, it would take too long.'

Hastily, he said, 'I will have my carriage brought round.'

She headed back to the door. 'I will be down shortly.'

'Not too long, Ju. It don't do the horses good to be kept waiting.'

'I know, George. You have told me repeatedly.'

Sebastian brought his greys to a halt in front of Lord Smythe-Clyde's townhouse. He had never been here before, but thought it best if he was seen around London with Juliet. It would make their engagement more believable.

The note he had sent her this morning asking her to go driving had elicited no answer. Never patient, he was here to bodily lift her into his phaeton if needed. The chit would not snub him.

He leapt down and strode to the door. Imperiously he banged the knocker. The door opened just as he pulled his hand away. Hobson stood in the doorway, looking down his nose.

Sebastian smothered a smile. The butler would not appreciate being found amusing.

'I am here to take Miss Smythe-Clyde driving.'

Hobson did not usher the Duke inside. 'Does Miss Juliet know you are coming?'

Sebastian frowned. 'She should. I sent round a note this morning.'

The butler looked flustered, but he maintained his ground. 'She is not available.' He moved to close the door.

Anger spurred Sebastian. He put his palm against the heavy oak and pushed. 'I will not be turned away. Show me to a place to wait and tell her I am here.'

By strength alone, Sebastian made his way inside. This was the last time the chit would treat him so cavalierly. Not waiting for Hobson to escort him, Sebastian strode across the hall and opened the first door he came to. It was the drawing room. He went in and sat down in the only comfortable-looking chair.

Minutes passed and no one came. He rose, determination hardening his jaw. No one had ever treated him this poorly. He would find where she was and drag her out. She needed to be taught a lesson.

His hand was on the doorknob when the door moved inward. He backed away. Harry stood in the archway, looking apprehensive.

'So she sent you,' Sebastian drawled, keeping his anger in check. 'I had not thought her a coward.'

Harry slid inside, keeping his face turned towards the Duke. 'Umm…she don't want to see you.'

'Do you always state the obvious?' Sebastian asked, wanting to draw blood.

Harry turned beet-red. Even his ears glowed. 'Ripping up at me won't do any good. *I* cannot make her do what she don't want. Nor can you,' he added for good measure.

'Your tongue is as sharp as hers.'

Tired of the verbal battle that was getting him nowhere, Sebastian went to the door and opened it. He walked into the entry and headed for the stairs.

'Hey,' Harry yelped, rushing after the Duke. 'What are you doing?'

Sebastian started up the steps. 'Use your brain. I am going after her.'

'You can't!' Harry pounded up the stairs and grabbed the Duke's arm.

Sebastian stopped and looked down at the youth. 'Take your hand off me,' he said, his voice deadly.

Harry blanched. His hand fell away. 'She ain't here,' he said, his voice barely audible.

Sebastian's eyes narrowed. He did not like the way this was going. 'Where is she?'

Harry looked around. Several servants were moving around in the hall. 'If you come back to the drawing room, I will tell you.'

Cold premonition stiffened Sebastian's spine. The chit had done something truly reprehensible this time. He just knew it.

Back in the privacy of the drawing room, he stared at Harry. 'Out with it.'

Harry paced the room, his fingers raking through his

hair in time to his feet. He would not meet the
Duke's fierce look. 'She's left.'

'I know that,' Sebastian said, his patience at an end.

'She went with George.'

'Who is George? And make it quick and thor-
ough. I am done putting up with your delaying tac-
tics. Your sister has gone too far this time.'

'Don't I just know that,' Harry mumbled, his feet
still moving. He took a deep breath and let it all out
at once. 'She eloped.'

'She did what?' Sebastian said, his voice low.

Harry was not fooled. He knew the Duke was
ready to throttle him, and heaven only knew what
he would do to Ju if he got hold of her. 'Eloped.
Gretna Green.'

'Bloody…' Sebastian ground his teeth together.
'And you did nothing?'

Harry swallowed, his Adam's apple bobbing con-
vulsively. 'George will not hurt her. He left a mes-
sage to be delivered to me. Seems he did not want
anyone to get worried.'

Disgust flared Sebastian's nostrils. 'And that
makes it all right?'

'Yes. I mean, no. That is, George is an old friend.
We grew up with him. He is like a brother.'

Sebastian could not believe the naïveté. 'You do
realise, don't you, that after what is being said about
your sister now an elopement will be the *coup de
grâce*. She will never be accepted anywhere, country

or town. I imagine she will even be shunned by your neighbours.'

Harry's eyes widened. 'Surely not.'

Sebastian shrugged. 'Perhaps. However, I do not intend to let your sister succeed in this harebrained scheme. She is too impetuous for her own good.'

'You are going to chase her?'

'Someone has to,' Sebastian said, wondering why he continued to put himself through this hell. If he had an ounce of self-preservation, he would send a retraction to the papers. He might be called a cad, but he had been called worse.

'Can I go with you? I won't be any trouble and I'm her brother. I should be there to protect her.' Harry's excitement made his hair seem to stand on end. 'Not from you… That is…'

Sebastian looked the youth up and down. He would be a complication, but he did have a point. There was enough impropriety in this mess which his inclusion might help blunt.

'We are riding horses. Quicker. I shall leave in half an hour. If you are not at my house, I will go without you. Is that clear?'

'Yes, sir…your Grace.'

Sebastian wasted no time getting home and to his chamber.

'A change of shirt and linen,' he told Roberts. 'I am leaving in fifteen minutes.'

'Shall I pack a portmanteau, your Grace?' the valet said, already pulling out the luggage.

'No, thank you. I shall be on horseback.'

'What?' A horrified expression filled the servant's face. 'Surely you jest. What will people say? You have a reputation to maintain. You are one of the best-dressed men in all of England.'

'Calm yourself, Roberts. No one of importance is going to see me. I am going into the country.'

'Yes, your Grace,' the valet said in a despondent tone. 'I shall have my own bag packed in a trice.'

'You are not coming.'

'What?'

'Close your mouth, Roberts, you look like a beached fish. I am travelling alone.'

The valet clamped his teeth so hard they clicked and he winced. Not a further word escaped him as he watched the Duke leave. But his head drooped.

Juliet sat across from George, the inn's best cherrywood table between them, and watched him eat and eat and eat. At the speed he was going they would be here until it was too dark to travel and the inn's larder was empty. She had finished long ago. She muffled an irritated sigh with her napkin.

He looked up from his mutton. 'Are you all right? We can stop the night here if you would like.'

She felt as if they were barely out of London and all its environs. The last thing she wanted was to stay here. 'No, I think it best that we continue on. You could have them pack that up for you,' she ended on a hopeful note.

'Capital idea. Should have thought of that myself.' He rang the little brass bell the innkeeper had left with them.

Soon they were on the road again. Juliet took a breath of the cool evening air and wished she were somewhere else. Anywhere except eloping. But there was no help for it.

George sat on the opposite side of the carriage, snoring. He had finished everything the innkeeper had wrapped and then promptly fallen asleep. At least she did not have to worry about poor dear George trying to seduce her or in any way embarrassing her with his overtures. She was not sure he had an amorous bone in his body, for which she was heartily glad.

How different it would be if Brabourne sat across from her. First, he would not be on the other seat, he would be beside her. She had no doubt that his sensuality would overwhelm any protests she might have. He was…he was…

She sighed and looked away from her companion. The Duke was everything George was not.

That, she told herself harshly, is why you will do better with good stolid George. He will let you run things the way you wish and not bother you. Brabourne would devour you and then bed other women. Infidelity is in his nature.

This was better by far. It had to be—this was her future.

Energy coursed through Sebastian as he urged his mount onwards. 'We are not far behind,' he said, the passing wind catching his words and flinging them back to Harry.

Harry lagged behind. Even the best horse-flesh Lord Smythe-Clyde had was no match for the Duke's.

Sebastian thought he saw a glimmer of light in the distance. It flickered and disappeared, only to reappear again. He was sure it belonged to a carriage.

Wait until he got his hands on the minx. He would teach her a lesson she would never forget. He would curb her impetuosity. No woman was going to leave him after the banns had been posted and the announcement put in the paper. He had declared his intentions to the world, and his pride and heritage demanded that she wed no one else. Especially not some country bumpkin.

They closed quickly on the vehicle. In the twilight, Sebastian could see the back of the coachman's head. There were no outriders. Stupid. They would pass through stretches where robberies occurred on a daily basis, sometimes multiple ones within twenty-four hours.

'By Jove,' Harry's voice rang out, 'that looks like George's old coach.'

Sebastian drew even with the first carriage horse and shouted to the coachman to stop. The servant slowed down, but before he could bring the vehicle to a complete stop Juliet popped her head out of the window.

She gasped. 'Brabourne! Coachman, don't stop. Speed up. This is the man we are running from.'

The servant only faltered for seconds. He knew whom he took his orders from. With a flick of the whip, he urged the four horses on. The carriage, old and large, lumbered behind the panting animals like an overfed cow.

Sebastian cursed under his breath. He was not afraid of losing them. He just wanted to put an end to this charade.

The carriage took a wide turn. One of its wheels hit a large rock. The coach tottered.

Sebastian heard a loud snap and the wheel that had hit the rock cracked. The vehicle skidded on the remaining three wheels until coming to an abrupt stop toppled to one side.

'Harry,' Sebastian yelled, jumping from his horse, 'go to their heads. They are panicking.'

To Sebastian's relief, the youth did as he was told without comment. While Harry tried to calm the horses Sebastian rushed to the carriage door and yanked it open.

Pandemonium reigned.

Juliet scrambled to regain her feet, only to fall down on to the lopsided cushion. Her companion looked dazed, as though he had hit his head. Several blankets littered the floor, which was now the other side of the coach. A wicker basket, with the lid open, lay at the door. The smell of baked chicken and fresh bread filled the interior. Chicken bones were sprinkled throughout as though a giant hand had deposited them.

Sebastian's gaze locked on to Juliet. 'Give me your hand and I will help you out.'

She shook her head.

'Now,' he said, his volume low, but with an underlining of iron.

She glanced at George, who merely looked confused. Seeing there was no help there, she grabbed the strap above the door and used it to pull herself to the opening. Sebastian caught her around the waist and swung her down before she could protest.

'I could have done it myself,' she said irritably, smoothing down the brown wool of her skirt. 'I am not helpless.'

She was stubborn and belligerent. Sebastian would have smiled under different circumstances, but the anger that had driven him to pursue her still held him.

'You,' he said coldly to the coachman, 'had best help your master. He looks as if he took a hit to the head.'

'Oh, dear,' Juliet said, edging past Sebastian and leaning her upper body inside the carriage. 'Are you all right, George? You were sleeping when the wheel broke.'

'Yes, yes,' he muttered. 'Just a bit confused.'

'Where is my reticule?' she said, starting to climb back into the vehicle. 'I have smelling slats. They will help.'

She had just put her left knee on the top of the carriage when Sebastian wrapped her arm around her and hauled her out. 'He will be fine without your ministrations. You are not going back in there. No telling what will happen next. This is a relic and should never have been on the road, let alone racing.'

Together with the coachman, Sebastian helped George out. The country squire sank to the ground. One glance at the poor man told Sebastian this was no love match.

Juliet grabbed a blanket from the vehicle and wrapped it around George. 'Is that better?'

He nodded.

Harry had the horses calmed and unharnessed. They were munching on grass by the side of the road. He came up to them and said, 'I think he needs a doctor.'

Sebastian ignored him and spoke to George. 'This is going to hurt, old man, but I want to feel around your head and find out where you bumped yourself.'

George groaned, then gasped sharply. 'Damme, that hurts.'

'Shine the carriage lamp on this,' Sebastian ordered. The coachman found an extra candle and lit it, then put it close enough for Sebastian to see. 'You've got a nasty bruise forming, but it is not bleeding much. You will have a knot the size of Prinny's waist by tomorrow.'

'I…I think I'm…going…' George did not finish.

Sebastian stepped away just in time. Juliet stared and managed to suppress her own sympathetic gag. Harry turned green.

'A wet cloth will do wonders,' Sebastian said laconically.

Juliet hastened to wet one of her handkerchiefs from the jug of water. She knelt by George and gingerly wiped his forehead.

'Not there,' Sebastian said. 'On his bump.'

She glared at him, but did as he directed.

Harry sidled up to Sebastian. 'How do you know so much?'

'Had my share of over-indulgence. Head wounds too.' Sebastian motioned to the coachman. 'I want you and Mr Smythe-Clyde to stay here with your master. Miss Smythe-Clyde and I are returning to the last inn to find a doctor and send help.'

Juliet jumped up, dropping the damp cloth. 'I will not go with you. I will stay here. George needs me.'

Sebastian looked from her face to the now dirty cloth. 'I doubt that.'

'You do, don't you, George?' she asked.

'I do,' George mumbled obediently.

Sebastian took hold of her arm and steered her towards his horse. 'You are coming with me, either in front of me on my horse or on Harry's mount. Which will it be?'

She stared stubbornly at him.

'As you wish.'

He gripped her around the waist and tossed her up. She landed with a bone-jarring thud in his saddle.

'You will have to ride astride so you don't fall off,' he said. 'Unless you promise to co-operate and let me balance you against my chest without fighting; then you may ride side-saddle.'

'You know I cannot ride astride,' she hissed.

He eyed her narrow skirt. 'I can remedy that. Coachman, do you have a knife?'

She gasped. 'You would not dare.'

He met her angry gaze with his cool one. This was almost worth the chase, he thought. She might be a hazard, and too impulsive for her or anyone else's own good, but she had spirit.

'Try me,' he said calmly, taking the knife from the servant.

'Harry,' she said, 'are you going to let him bully me like this?'

For the first time in his life, her brother did nothing to help. 'Deuced stupid thing you did, eloping and all. Even if I don't think his Grace is the husband for you, I don't think a flight to Gretna Green just days before your wedding is the thing either.'

She frowned at him. 'Should I have stood Brabourne up at the chapel? For I would have.'

Harry shook his head. 'I still think you could have talked Papa around.'

She looked away from him, and Sebastian would have sworn he saw a tear slide down her cheek in the dim glow of the lantern. He almost felt sorry for her. But she had gone too far this time.

'You win,' she said softly.

He handed the knife back to the coachman and mounted behind her. Taking the reins in one hand, he wrapped his other arm around her waist.

'It should not be above an hour,' he told the three men.

Juliet shivered as Brabourne set the horse in motion. The evening was cool and her pelisse was more fashionable than practical.

Brabourne held her pinned to his chest as though he expected her to try and get away. Not much chance of that. She recognised defeat when it sat behind her.

The heat from his body penetrated the clothing

separating them. It felt good. Too good. She stiffened and tried to put distance between them.

He hauled her back.

'You are cold,' he said. 'Staying close will help.'

'I don't want your help,' she said.

'Just as you don't want my name and title,' he said harshly.

'Exactly.'

His grip tightened painfully, squeezing the air out of her lungs. Then he loosened his hold. She sensed that his reaction had been automatic. She did not think he would intentionally hurt her, not physically.

'You will have both,' he said. 'The banns have been read, the announcement is in the paper, the church is reserved, your dress is made and the invitations are out. There is no turning back. Nor are you going to botch it all by running off with some squire's stolid son.'

Anger and the urge to hurt him as she knew he would eventually hurt her drove her. 'He is twice the man you are. Ten times. A hundred times,' she said defiantly, her voice rising. 'You are nothing but a rake and a libertine who has wealth and position. I despise you for what you are.'

He reined the horse to an abrupt halt that would have sent her tumbling to the ground if not for his hold on her. He slid down and pulled her with him so that their bodies bonded.

She felt everything about him. The silver buttons

on his coat scraped against her belly and then her breast, sending sensations skittering down her spine. His arms banded her waist and back like iron, and his chest crushed hers. He held her body immobile against the length of his. It was wickedly thrilling and frighteningly comfortable, as though she were meant to be this close to him.

She was going crazy.

'Let me go.'

'Not yet,' he replied, gripping the back of her head with one hand.

She stared up at him, anxiety twisting her stomach. It had to be anxiety, she told herself as his face lowered to hers. She did not want him to kiss her. Never again.

'You are an infuriating minx,' he said, just before his lips met hers.

The kiss was hard and punishing, not gentle and coaxing like the first. This one seared.

His mouth slanted across hers, and when she would not grant his tongue entry he nipped her bottom lip so that she gasped. He took instant advantage. He plundered her, swamping her senses with his sensual onslaught.

She reeled, and would have collapsed if not for his support.

'When I am done,' he vowed, 'you won't want that man you say is worth a hundred of me.'

His kiss gentled just before he broke away to nuz-

zle the hollow at the base of her throat. His tongue
flicked against her skin. The hand that had held her
head slid down and pushed the collar of her pelisse
aside to give him better access.

She gasped when his hand cupped her breast
through her clothing. Even with the barrier, she felt
as though he touched her bare skin. Her mind reeled.

'Stop,' she gasped.

He looked down at her, the light from the moon
and stars more than enough for her to see him
clearly. His eyes were a brilliant blue, seemingly lit
from within. His mouth was sensual in its hardness.

She gazed at him and saw hunger in every line
of his face. She exulted in her power to arouse him
like that, even as she feared what he would do to
her. He would make her want him.

His lips found hers again. His hand caressed her
breast, making her nipple peak. His arm pressed her
tightly against his hips so that she felt every hard
angle of him.

She was doomed.

She felt his fingers on the button running down
the back of her dress and a traitorous disappointment
filled her. He would never be able to undo them.
Not now. Not like this.

One. Two. Three… They opened under his fingers. The only thing keeping the garment from sliding down her shoulders was the pelisse she still
wore. Soon she felt the heat of his palms moving

inside the shoulders of her pelisse and edging it down her arms. All the while he held her captive with the power of his kiss.

The pelisse fell to the ground and the cool night air moved across her exposed back. Then the bodice slipped from her shoulders and Brabourne took his mouth from hers and placed it at the swell just above her bosom.

She shuddered at the moist warmth of his lips. One of his hands cupped her breast, easing it out of her chemise. His thumb flicked the aroused nipple as he raised his head and watched her reaction. She licked her lips and heard him groan.

Her head dropped back to be supported by his arm around her shoulders. He bent his head until his tongue replaced his thumb. She moaned, shock and pleasure twinning into a knot centred in her abdomen. She arched against him.

He was destroying all her resistance as though it was nothing.

Her bodice hung around her hips, followed by the top of her chemise. She was bare to his perusal, allowing him to plunder from her head to her waist. He cupped her breasts with his hands and took turns nuzzling and sucking them with his mouth until she no longer knew where she ended and he began.

The world swirled around her.

It was a cold shock when he once more raised up to look at her. 'You are more beautiful than I imagined,' he said, his voice raspy, as though too long unused.

She gazed up at him, no longer caring what else he did to her. It would all be mind-and body-exploding.

She sucked in air, more aware of him than she had ever been of anything in her life. She clung to him, her fingers tangled in the folds of his coat.

'You are more skilful than I ever imagined,' she managed to say between lips swollen from his kisses. 'I never thought seduction would feel this way. No wonder Emily wants you.'

He released her so quickly she stumbled and fell to the hard ground. He turned from her and walked away to stand head resting on the trunk of a nearby tree. Stunned, she sat still for long moments.

'What did I do?' she finally managed to say, her voice coming out small and unsure. Belatedly, she realised she sounded like a timid little mouse.

He kept his back to her. 'Do not ever again mention your stepmother to me. I did not seduce her.' He turned back and strode to her, towering above. 'Do you understand?'

His anger was like a slap in the face. She scrambled to her feet, reality returning with a vengeance. What a weak fool she had been.

She stuffed her arms back into the chemise and yanked it up over her breasts, trying to make it reach her chin. She shoved her arms into the sleeves of her bodice and contorted like an acrobat in a futile attempt to button the back. Tears of frustration and shame blurred her vision. She angled away so he would not see her weakness.

Stupid, stupid, stupid. She had been a complete fool. He had done nothing to her that he had not done to a million other women, and she had let him. No, she had revelled in his ardour.

He touched her shoulder and she jumped away. 'Don't come near me,' she ordered.

She heard him sigh, but when he spoke his voice was stripped of emotion. 'You will never be able to do up your bodice by yourself.'

'I shall do the best I can, for you shan't touch me again. I promise you that.'

His voice hardened. 'Don't make promises you cannot keep.'

'Where is my pelisse?' she muttered, looking around. The brown wool made the garment hard to see against the dirt. 'Ah.' She pounced on it and yanked it on, hoping it was long enough to cover most of the exposed skin of her back.

'You look unkempt,' his hateful voice said. 'As though you have been ravished and enjoyed every minute of it.'

She scowled, her resentment of her weakness and his skill rising to uncontrollable heights. She rounded on him. 'And you are a philanderer. A seducer of innocent women. A rakehell.'

He sneered. 'I have heard "rake" from your lips more than I like. Is your vocabulary so limited that you can think of nothing else?'

She lunged for him, her open palm connecting with his cheek. The instant her flesh met his, she knew he had let her hit him. The knowledge was in his bitter eyes.

The fury left her. 'I am sorry. I lost control, something I never do.'

His laugh was cynical. 'You do it all the time. Whenever you act impulsively you are losing control.'

Much to her dismay, he was right. It was her greatest weakness. Mama had told her so often enough. And now it had landed her in this bumble-broth from which she finally acknowledged to herself there was no escape.

'You are right,' she said in a tiny voice. 'I should never have fought you in that duel. Look where it has taken us, what it has done to us. I should have found another way to protect Papa.'

'You should have let him fight his own battle.'

'Oh, no, I could never do that. I promised Mama that I would care for him. And I shall.'

'What nonsense,' he said.

'It is a promise. I keep my promises.'

He studied her. 'And will you keep your promises on our wedding day?'

She blanched. 'You are a cunning devil, turning my words against me.'

He shrugged. 'Enough, minx. I am tired, and I venture so are you. We still have to reach that inn and send someone back for the others.

She had forgotten all else in the wonder of his lovemaking. Disgust at herself gave her energy. Briskly, she said. 'You are right.'

This time she co-operated with him when he mounted and pulled her up in front of him. She felt the tension in him when her shoulder touched his chest, but she told herself to ignore it. Just as she had to ignore her reaction to him.

She was, beyond question, a fool. Soon to be a hurt one.

Chapter Ten

For the second time since coming to London, Juliet returned home from Brabourne's protection. This time, however, Harry accompanied her and they arrived in George's carriage, which had been repaired speedily because of the Duke's intervention.

She was glad Brabourne had not come with them. After what had happened between them she never wanted to see him again. A forlorn wish. He had made it plain that he intended their wedding to take place and would brook no further evasions on her part. Nor would she get the chance for another. Her papa would have her watched, or rather Emily would. Papa never stayed focused on anything for long except his experiments.

George left them at the door and went on to his rented lodgings. No words were said between any of them.

She and Harry were met inside by Emily and Papa

and marched into the library. Anger at the other woman's obvious influence mixed with Juliet's sense of guilt over having been the cause of discomfort for Papa. Her job was to care for him, not upset him.

Harry looked at her and rolled his eyes. She nearly smiled at him, but remembered she was still angry. It was his fault Brabourne had caught her. She turned away, prepared to face the consequences without his help.

'How dare you, you ungrateful brat?' Emily started. Papa put a restraining hand on his wife's arm which she shook off. 'No, Oliver, I won't be denied my say. She has completely undone everything I have accomplished. She was about to marry Brabourne. Brabourne, the most sought-after man in all the realm. And she runs away. Not only is she ungrateful, she is stupid.'

Juliet stood stoically, but her stomach churned. The only thing that kept her standing was the knowledge that she had tried to do what was right for her. Brabourne was not the man for her, no matter how much her body responded to his and her weak emotions desired his nearness.

Emily continued her tirade.

Papa just shook his head, as though the entire situation bewildered him. It probably did. Finally he asked, 'Why, Juliet?'

'I don't want to marry him, Papa. He will make me miserable.'

'Then why didn't you say something instead of running away with poor George? It is not done. His father will be furious with him.'

She blinked rapidly, hoping no one saw the moisture in her eyes. This was so hard. Not even knowing she had been wrong eased the ache. 'I tried, Papa. You would not listen to me.'

'Of course I did, but you were wrong. Emily is right when she says this is for the best. You are ruined otherwise. No man will marry you.'

Juliet's stomach twisted again. 'George would have. Still will.'

She longed to tell Papa everything, particularly Emily's part, but for once controlled her tongue. It would do no good and only hurt Papa.

'You are too young and inexperienced,' Emily said in a condescending voice.

Juliet glared at her. 'I am three and twenty, nearly as old as you. And I may be inexperienced in the ways of the *ton,* but I am not ignorant of people.'

Emily raised on elegant blonde brow. 'Is that so? You have an odd way of showing it.'

Juliet sighed and looked away. There was nothing else to say. But it hurt just the same. If Mama were alive, none of this would be happening. But she was not.

'Go to your room,' Emily ordered. 'And be assured that you will not get a second opportunity to so disgrace us. Fortunately for you no one realises what really happened.'

Juliet cast one last imploring glance at Papa, who looked bewildered as he shook his head. She turned and left the room. Harry followed, the tread of his boots loud in the stilled house. He stayed behind her.

Reaching her door, she turned to him. 'Please go away. I know all you want to do is agree with *her*.'

He ran his fingers through his red hair. 'I'm sorry, Ju. I didn't mean for it to be this bad. Just…you just cannot run away with someone to avoid someone else. It isn't done.'

'Some of the most high-ranking people in the aristocracy have eloped,' she hissed. 'And I don't care. George and I would never even have come to London.'

He sighed. 'Those runaway marriages were mostly in our grandparents' time, Ju. People don't do it so much now. At least, not respectable ones.'

His words piled more pain on. 'But you forget,' she said sarcastically, 'I am no longer respectable.'

Her neck ached from stiffness and tension. Soon she would have a raging headache. She rubbed the stiff muscles.

'Please, Harry, just go away. I need time to myself.'

She could see his uncertainty, but he did as she asked. With feet that dragged, she entered her room and crossed to the bed. She crawled on to the large mattress and curled up, staring at nothing.

She was trapped now. No other chance to escape Brabourne would present itself. Emily would gain admittance to the select of Society. She would see some doors open and others remain closed. She might even become an intimate of Prinny. She did not care.

She rolled on to her back.

Then there was Brabourne. She did not want to marry him. Not really. Or so she told herself. He would break her heart. Perhaps he already had, if the pain in her chest was any indication.

She rolled to her other side and squeezed her eyes shut against the tears she had managed to hold in until now. They soaked her pillow.

When had it happened? How could it have happened?

There had been times when he had been kind to her. He had not shot Papa in the duel, even though he could have. That alone had endeared him to her against her better judgement. Then he had rescued her from the thugs in Vauxhall. But those events should not have captured her heart.

Yes, he made her body throb with pleasure and sensations she had never known existed. But that should not have been enough either.

Mama had once said that love was never logical

and never comfortable. Perhaps she had been right.
Look what it had done to Papa.

To her.

A week later, Juliet stepped down from the travelling carriage Brabourne had sent for her family.
Brabourne Abbey, the seat of the Dukes of Brabourne, was stupendous. A large, rambling abbey in
the Gothic style, acquired when Henry VIII had dissolved the monasteries, it had been in the family
ever since. The grey rock blended in with the cliff
on which it perched, the English Channel visible
from all the south-and east-facing rooms.

To Juliet's mind it suited Brabourne perfectly.
Dark and arrogant.

She had not taken three steps from the carriage
before footmen in the Duke's green and black livery
were there to assist. Brabourne was right behind
them.

'Welcome to my home, Juliet,' he said, taking the
hand she had not offered. Watching her the entire
time, he kissed her fingers.

Even though she wore gloves, the feel of his lips
was distinct and unsettling. Memories flooded back
of their minutes in the dark night. Her pulse raced
and her heart pounded. She could not look away
from his knowing eyes.

'I believe Prinny was right. You will set a new
fashion for freckles, my dear,' he said *sotto voce*.

The spell broke and she snatched her hand back. 'I seriously doubt that. No one likes freckles. They are too much like blemishes.'

Before he could further discompose her, she turned away. Emily and Papa exited the coach with Harry close behind. The carriage that carried their luggage drew up and more servants converged on it. It was organised mayhem.

Brabourne welcomed her papa. 'Come this way, Smythe-Clyde. My butler and housekeeper will show you to your accommodations.'

'Yes, yes,' Papa said, his gaze darting all around. 'Nice place you have here, Brabourne. If it were mine, I should never go to the city.'

Emily rolled her eyes. 'Oliver, don't be ridiculous.'

The small group headed to the marble steps that led to the front door. Juliet lagged behind, marvelling that Papa was acting as though he had never challenged the Duke to a duel. Men were so strange. Or Papa was.

She was not surprised to see Burroughs waiting for them. Not even with the blink of an eye did he reveal that he knew her. He assigned a footman to show Harry to his room and took Papa and Emily to theirs himself. Juliet was left standing in the entry with Brabourne.

Old muskets adorned the walls in circles like radiating suns. Many-antlered deer gazed down at them with sightless eyes. The Brabourne crest and motto, a jousting knight and the words *Never Fear*, were emblazoned above the entryway. Soon they would be hers too.

'Not nearly so ornate as Carlton House,' the Duke said drily.

'Not enough gilt,' she managed to remark with a slight smile.

'I will take you to your chamber,' he said abruptly. 'Come with me.' He held out his arm.

The ease that had started to slow her pulse ended. She glanced apprehensively up at him. He stood implacably, waiting. Juliet knew when she was up against a wall. With ill grace, she accepted his escort.

The muscles of his lower arm were sinewy and strong beneath her fingers. She knew their power from his rescue and his lovemaking, thoughts she did not want to have at this moment.

They progressed up a flight of stairs wide enough for three ladies to walk three abreast while wearing the wide skirts of a generation ago. Gleaming marble overlaid with a fine red carpet stretched ahead. Periodically they passed a footman, who bowed until they were past. It was overdone and overwhelming.

'You are like a potentate here,' Juliet said, hard pressed to keep the distaste from her voice.

'Do I detect displeasure? You will have to get

used to this. Anything less would not be fitting for my station.'

Was there bitterness in his last words? She looked at him as they walked. His face, as usual, was un-revealing.

They stopped in front of two double doors with the Brabourne crest and motto carved across them. She got a strange feeling in her stomach.

With his free hand, Brabourne opened the doors. Juliet gazed into a room big enough to be a ballroom in many houses.

He ushered her in, leaving the doors open. 'This is your sitting room. Beyond is the sleeping chamber and a room for your maid.'

Done in shades of pale green and black, the Bra-bourne colours, it was enough to take her breath away. A settee and several chairs grouped around a table where tea had been laid out. A large secretary and several bookcases took up part of one wall. The wood floor was covered in carpet. Many-paned win-dows, with green brocade curtains with black trim pulled back, presented the view of a stormy English Channel. She imagined that during a storm she would hear the waves pound the shore.

'Magnificent,' she breathed.

'It is the suite of rooms traditionally occupied by the Duchess. My rooms are connected through a door in your sleeping chamber.'

She was not surprised. Even a house as grand as

this could not have many rooms this fantastic. Still, he was bucking respectability by putting her here before their marriage.

He must have known her thoughts. 'By tomorrow it will no longer matter. I am tired of being dictated to by narrow minds.'

There was nothing she could say. She was not yet mistress here. Besides, a large part of her agreed with him. She was heartily tired of having her life tossed about because of what others expected.

'I will leave you now,' he said, releasing her. 'We keep country hours here, in spite of Prinny's presence, but we do dress. The dinner bell will ring at five.'

'Prinny is here?' She had known he was close to Brabourne, and that he intended to attend the wedding, but she had thought he would arrive tomorrow.

'He came several days ago. He likes the hunting.'

The Duke's voice was non-committal and Juliet wondered what else the Prince liked. But it was none of her business.

'We will be twenty for dinner,' he added as he left.

Juliet stood looking at the closed doors long after he had gone. Twenty might be small for him, but to her it was too many. The day had been long and the preceding weeks even longer. Tomorrow was her wedding day, the ceremony to be held in the estate chapel. She really did not want to spend the evening trying to appear excited and eager.

A knock on the door signalled the arrival of her trunks. More would follow over the next week or so. Striding into her sleeping chamber and seeing the massive wardrobe and tallboy, and a separate room specially designed for her gowns, Juliet began to wonder if she had enough clothing for the life she was entering into. She would worry about that later. Right now she needed to direct the unpacking and find a gown suitable for tonight's activities. Pleading sick on the eve of her wedding was not the thing to do.

Several hours later, she studied herself in the large bevelled mirror. She wore the same bronze silk gown she had worn to Almack's, with the same single strand of pearls. Gold ribbon threaded through the curls her maid had let fall like autumn leaves on to her shoulders from a gold clasp on top of her head. Something was missing.

She looked like a schoolgirl. The last thing she wanted. It had not bothered her before, but now she felt gauche in these magnificent surroundings. Out of her depth.

And, a small part of her acknowledged, she wanted to stand out so that Brabourne would notice her and admire her. As much as she told herself she did not want to marry him, she still wanted him to be proud of her. For what reason, she could not, would not admit to herself. The need was just there, nestled in her chest and demanding satisfaction.

She sighed and stood. This was silly.

The smooth sound of wood sliding on wood alerted her. The door to Brabourne's room opened. He stood in the entryway, watching her, a velvet box in one hand.

He was magnificent, everything she had ever dreamed a man should be. There was a powerful grace about him when he moved, showing his lean body to advantage. His longish hair brushed his shoulders, its darkness nearly lost in the midnight colour of his coat. Black breeches moulded to him.

She gulped and looked away.

'I have something for you,' he said, stopping too close for her comfort.

He flicked open the box and held it out to her. On a bed of black velvet lay a necklace that caught the candlelight and split it into many shades of yellow, orange and red. It was a choker made up of three strands with a large, canary-yellow oval stone in the centre. Around it was a circle of red stones with an orange tinge. More yellow stones made up the three strands. It was stunning. Matching earrings and bracelets lay beside it.

'I have never seen anything so…so striking,' she said.

'They are the Brabourne diamonds. The centre

stone is one of the largest yellow diamonds in existence. They will look good on you.'

She looked from the jewels to him. 'I cannot wear them. What if I lost them?'

'You are impossible. I had them cleaned and the catch strengthened. The settings are also good.' He took the necklace out and set the box on a table. 'You will not lose them unless you get into a skirmish with someone, which I don't expect tonight.' A slight smile curved his lips. 'To my knowledge, there are no thugs present.'

She returned his smile with a grimace. 'One never knows.'

'True. You are prone to finding trouble. Now, turn around so I can hook this.'

She looked at him, noting the implacable gaze he bent on her. No argument would sway him. That much she had learned about him. With a reluctant sigh, she did as he ordered.

His fingers brushed the nape of her neck just seconds before her pearls slid down so that one end came to rest where the fabric of her bodice ended. The smooth feel of pearl slid along her skin as he pulled them free. The breath she had not realised she held slipped through her parted lips.

She had barely regained her composure when his fingers once more touched her. A *frisson* shot down her spine. The cool kiss of diamonds and gold rested against the heated flush of her reaction to him.

For a fleeting instant she thought she felt his lips against her neck and across her exposed shoulder. Shivers joined the *frisson* that continued to move through her. Then he stepped away.

'Turn around so that I may see you,' he said, his voice a harsh sound in the utter silence.

She did as she was told, unable to do otherwise. His voice held the same sound it had the night he had nearly ravished her. When she saw him, the hunger in his gaze took her aback.

He reached out and with one finger traced the line of the necklace. Where his flesh met hers fire erupted. He bent forward and kissed the base of her throat, just below the centre diamond. She moaned in shocked surprise and delight, her fingers reaching out to grasp something so she would not fall. Her nails dug into the fabric covering of the chair behind her.

He raised his head and stared down at her. Her chest rose and fell in small panting gasps.

'They become you,' he murmured. 'I knew they would.'

She stared at him, her eyes wide with reaction while his were slumberous. If he crooked his finger, she would fall willingly into his arms. It was a shameful admission, but she knew it for the truth.

She was his—body and soul.

Instead, he stepped further away. 'We must go down. Our guests are waiting.'

Disappointment made its insidious way through her emotions. She caught herself up short with a shake of the head. Would she never learn?

'You are right,' she said, her voice remarkably level for the turmoil her thoughts were in.

Holding her head high, she preceded him through the door. After his bestowal of the jewels, anything else would be anti-climactic.

She was right.

The next morning, Juliet stood across the altar from her groom in the small chapel situated on the Brabourne estate. This was not her choice of place, but Brabourne had thought it best after her attempted elopement. Behind them stood her family, Prinny and Perth. Ravenswood stood as groomsman to Brabourne. She had no bridesmaid.

George had not been invited.

In half an hour all the rich and powerful who were not already here would be arriving for the wedding breakfast.

Right now, she had to turn to the Duke and allow him to kiss her. Her hands shook, so she hid them in the folds of her white silk and silver lace gown. Please let it be chaste. She did not want to succumb to him in front of these people. She never wanted to melt against him again.

He touched his lips to her cheek before holding his arm out for her hand. Relief flooded her. She laid her fingers lightly on him and hoped he did not feel her shivers.

He graciously accepted congratulations, even smiling at his friends and the Prince. She managed to keep her lips parted in what she hoped looked like a smile. It was the best she could do.

'Beautiful bride, you lucky devil,' Prinny said with a wink.

Before Juliet realised what the prince intended, he planted his mouth full on hers. She gasped, but managed to keep from jumping back. She could not stop the blush.

'Thank you, Your Highness,' she said, grateful her voice did not tremble.

'Oh, Your Highness,' Emily cooed, having come up beside him, 'you are such a charming rogue.'

He took her hand and beamed down at her. Together they left the chapel. Juliet glanced at her papa, who stood to one side watching.

'Why don't you ask him to go in with us?' Brabourne said quietly.

Juliet gave her new husband a speaking look, torn equally between gratitude for his kindness and irritation that he was so thoughtful, which weakened her resolve to dislike him. She could not control her heart, but she was determined to control her mind.

She rushed to Papa, only to have Harry get there first. 'Come with us,' she said to both of them.

Harry grinned and shook his head. 'We will follow. This is your moment—and your husband's.'

She frowned at him, but knew from the stubborn
light in his eyes that he would not change his mind.
With ill grace, she returned to the Duke, who once
more held out his arm.

'You can do better than that,' he chided, his face
once more masked by his cool reserve. 'After all the
trouble we have gone to, there is no sense in de-
feating our purpose by having the tongues wagging
that our marriage is a sham.'

'Why should they think anything else?' she
hissed. 'Everyone knows you only married me to
save my reputation.'

He shrugged. 'That does not mean you have to
confirm their suspicions. They can just as easily believe it is a love match. After all, I compromised
you. Let them guess.'

She gave an unladylike snort.

They entered the large ballroom that Brabourne
had had made into a bower of flowers. Through the
many french windows she saw white silk tents set
up on the acres of lawn. Beneath them were more
tables laden with food. Her husband had spared no
expense.

People were everywhere, dressed in the height of
fashionable morning dress. She had to endure the
next couple hours and into the evening. Many of the

important guests had arrived last night and stayed over.

Brabourne led her to the largest table, where a many-layered bride's cake reposed. His French chef had been working on it for days. Crystal, china and silver sparkled like constellations around it. With luck, she could spend the rest of the morning and early afternoon cutting the cake.

Then there was the night.

Chapter Eleven

Juliet could stand the waiting no longer. With a huff of ire, she jumped out of the massive four-poster bed and marched to the mantel. She grabbed a brass poker from the stand and attacked the coals. Heat jumped out at her from the reinvigorated fire. It was small satisfaction.

This was her wedding night and she had come to bed hours ago, or so it seemed to her heightened nerves. Many of the guests had left that afternoon. The only ones remaining were her family, Prinny, Perth and Ravensford. She had left Brabourne drinking with his cronies, thinking he would soon follow.

She was a fool.

She returned the poker to its stand and went to the large window. Pulling the curtains back, she peered out at the night. Clouds scuttled across the sky, obscuring the stars. The moon was only a sliver. If she listened hard enough, she could hear the waves hitting the rocky shores. This was a primitive, vital land, like its owner.

She let the curtain close. Some hot chocolate would be nice, and might help her to sleep, but she did not want to let anyone know of her shame. Her husband was not interested enough in her to come and do his duty. She must have been mistaken when she'd thought she saw hunger on his face after he had fastened the diamonds around her throat.

Her temples began to throb.

Everyone had gasped the night before when they had entered the salon. Emily had turned green. The large gilt mirror over the mantel had shown her the necklace sparkling like a miniature sun around her neck. She had been beautiful, if only because of the jewels. She had even felt beautiful for the first time in her life.

Now, the diamonds were back in their case on her dressing stand. She was back to her normal self.

She returned to the bed, crawled in and burrowed under the covers. It might be summer, but being so close to water kept the abbey too cool for comfort. She turned into the embrace of the fluffy pillows and told herself she was better off without Brabourne in her bed. He was too expert at what he did to leave her unscathed.

Sebastian paused at the door separating his room from Juliet's. He had drunk everyone under the table and now felt a cool detachment about his new wife. The desire that had driven him lurked beneath the haze caused by good French wine. Yet he knew that if he crossed the wooden barrier separating them, all his good intentions would be for naught. He would have her to wife and be damned to anything else.

The cynical part of him said do it. He would ensure her first child was his.

The side of himself he showed only to those few people close to him said wait. For her first time with a man she deserved to have someone who was sober enough to give her pleasure and to care about how she felt. Right now he was not that person.

He should not have drunk so much, trying to exorcise the spectre of his mother and her infidelity to the man the world had known as his father. His marriage had opened wide the already-weeping wound of his bastardy. Telling himself Juliet was not his mother did no good. Juliet was a woman, and he did not trust women.

Hands clenched, shoulders tight, he turned and went to his bed. He snuffed the single candle he carried and set it on the side table, then undid the sash of his navy robe and let the silk slither to the floor. Naked, he got under the cold covers.

It was going to be a long night.

The next morning Juliet rose before the maid came to her room and made her bed. Raised in the country, she knew the first servant in to tidy the room would realise she and Brabourne had not consummated their marriage. She had never thought herself prideful, but having people know her husband could not bring himself to make love to her on their wedding night was more than she could bear.

She pulled the bell; when a footman came, she told him she wanted Mrs Burroughs. It was not so strange a request for a new bride. Brabourne had introduced her to the staff yesterday after their marriage. It was plausible that she intended to speak to the housekeeper about the running of the abbey…what if it was a little too early? She was eccentric.

Mrs Burroughs arrived promptly, making a curtsy to Juliet. 'Your Grace?'

'Please, Mrs Burroughs, don't treat me that way. I am not used to it.'

The housekeeper smiled warmly. 'Used to it or not, you are a Duchess now and must learn to accept what comes with it.'

Juliet wrung her hands and paced the floor of her chamber. How did one go about asking for help to hide this sort of thing? If only Ferguson or Hobson were here.

Reaching the sticking point, she stopped short and blurted, 'Mrs Burroughs, I need your help. The Duke did not visit me last night.' Embarrassment was like a flame that burned her face.

The old woman's round cheeks turned ruddy even as sympathy softened the lines around her eyes. 'Oh, dear. I knew he would have problems, but I was so sure he was attracted to you enough that he would… Well, anyway. We must get you dressed, and you need to go to the Long Gallery to see the pictures. That will tell you. Meanwhile, I will tidy your room. No one must know what did not happen last night. Least of all your stepmother.'

Relief eased the constriction in Juliet's chest. She had found an ally. She dressed in a pale lavender morning dress, with a white paisley shawl around her shoulders to ward off the morning chill. Mrs Burroughs gave her directions to the Long Gallery and she set off, wondering what she was supposed to learn that Mrs Burroughs did not want to tell her.

She got lost twice, and finally asked a footman to show her the way. The young man made her a very impressive bow, which made her more uncomfortable. She was going to have trouble getting used to her new rank. At her destination he bowed again.

'Please,' she said, then stopped herself. She could not tell him to stop bowing. 'Thank you.'

He raised one eyebrow, but otherwise managed to keep an impassive face as he took his leave. Her impetuosity had nearly got her into trouble again. Being a Duchess was going to be hard work.

Drawing the shawl close, she started slowly walking the length of the room and studying the portraits as she went. The style of clothing changed with each painting, as did the women. Each Duchess differed from the one before or after her. Blonde, brown or black hair, and blue, brown or grey eyes, graced the women randomly. Some were plump and others thin. Some were tall and others short.

The men never seemed to change. Their clothes reflected the time period, but their features and bearing never altered. All the Dukes had blond hair and heavily lidded pale blue eyes. Their noses were arrogant hooks that turned down at the tip. Their lips were thin. Even the last Duke, Brabourne's father, looked like all those who had gone before him.

She stopped at the end of the gallery and studied the portraits of the last Duke and Duchess. The Duchess looked like Brabourne, the same raven-black hair and piercing blue eyes. Her lips were full and sensual like her son's. Her nose was straight and well defined and, like her son's, had no hook. She was willowy and he was lean. Brabourne had a squarer jaw, but that was the only major difference.

Juliet felt a presence and turned to see her husband. He stopped beside her and looked up at the picture of his mother.

'We are much alike.'

There was a harshness to his voice and an intensity to his body that told Juliet he was disturbed. He glanced down at her and his eyes were hard.

'I don't look anything like the last Duke.'

'Your father,' she said, before realisation hit her. She had been so stupid.

He stiffened. 'The man the world calls my father.'

Instinctively she reached for him. He moved as though to look somewhere else and managed to avoid her touch. She drew back, hurt.

'I have his name and title, but I am really a bastard,' he said softly.

She did not know what to say, but had to do something. The gulf between them was widening. 'You cannot know that for sure.'

'He told me.'

'Oh.'

'I was ten. It was my birthday. He never forgave my mother for doing it to him, and he never forgave me for living. I never forgave her either.' His voice was void of emotion, as though he spoke of someone else.

Juliet was appalled by the pain the last Duchess had wrought. She longed to comfort Brabourne, but did not think he would let her.

'I am so sorry,' she whispered, knowing the words were inadequate.

He turned back to her. 'Don't be. It is in the past.'

'But not forgotten or overcome.' Even as she said the words she knew she spoke the truth. When he said he had never forgiven his mother, he also meant he did not trust women. 'I will not do that to you, to our children.'

He looked at her for long minutes, then walked away without saying a word. Her heart ached for him as she watched his proud back disappear around a corner. Her heart ached for herself. She had known her marriage was far from perfect, but she had never imagined there was so much past pain that had to be put to rest before they could start to make the best of their life together.

One step at a time, she told herself. He would never love her, but she would make him trust her. She could live with that. She would have to.

For dinner that night she wore the palest of lavender. Brabourne sent her a magnificent set of amethyst and diamond jewellery. Her maid fastened the necklace. Juliet missed the electrifying sensuality of her husband's touch even as she wondered what maggot had taken up residence in her brain. She should be glad he was keeping his distance. It was what she had wanted from the beginning.

The Prince was still with them. During the meat course, he announced, 'I will be returning to London tomorrow, Brabourne. I hope to see you there after your wedding trip.'

'Within the week,' Brabourne answered without looking at Juliet.

No one said a word about there not being a trip.

'Really?' Emily said, 'Oliver and I were just talking about when we were returning to town. We have decided to go tomorrow as well.'

Juliet watched her papa, noting the look of confusion on his face.

Harry said, 'That is news to me. The hunting here is excellent, and Papa likes hunting above everything except his experiments.'

'Don't be ridiculous,' Emily said quickly. 'Oliver wants to get back to his experiments, don't you?'

'Yes, yes. Quite, m'dear.' He returned his attention to his meal.

Juliet watched her stepmother and wondered just what the other woman was up to. She had used Juliet's connections to Brabourne to better her position in Society. Was she now going to use her budding acquaintance with the Prince to further boost her position? Was Prinny aware?

Prinny smiled warmly at Emily. 'Delightful to have you coming back so soon, Lady Smythe-Clyde. The two of you must come to Carlton House.'

Juliet glanced at her husband. Brabourne was watching the exchange with a jaundiced air. He obviously knew something was going on between the Prince and Emily and did not approve. Papa seemed oblivious, his food holding all his attention.

What a mess, Juliet decided, grateful dinner was essentially over. She signalled for herself and Emily to leave the men with their port.

Her relief at escaping the quickly deteriorating dinner was short-lived.

With an insinuating tone, Emily asked, 'Was last night everything you thought it would be? Brabourne is reputed to be the best lover in England.'

Juliet's hated blush came in full force. Pulling herself together, she gave Emily a supercilious stare. 'How unladylike a question.'

Emily's eyes narrowed. 'High in the instep, now that you are a Duchess.' She moved nearer and said in a venomous whisper, 'But don't expect him every night. He has a reputation. No woman has ever held him exclusively.' Her tinkling laugh filled the room as she went to the sideboard and poured herself a glass of sherry.

Juliet left while the other woman's back was turned. She would not stay and hear Emily's bold words and hurtful insinuations. The truth in them was something she did not want to face tonight.

In her own rooms, she quickly dressed for bed. Her last request to her maid was for a cup of hot chocolate. She intended to sleep.

An hour later she sighed and threw the covers off. She got out of bed and lit the candle left near. By its golden glow she found her lavender wool robe and donned it, tying the sash tightly. She should have known oblivion would evade her.

A chill hung in the room. She crossed to the fireplace and stirred the banked coals. Sparks jumped up and rode the air currents like fairies. She smiled, remembering the tales of little people her nanny used to regale her and Harry with before bed.

A click and the smooth slide of a door across carpet froze her, poker in right hand. Very careful not to appear startled, she put the tool back, then pivoted around.

She swallowed hard.

Brabourne was a dark figure in the entry, the glow of the fire barely reaching him. He stood there, watching her for long moments before stepping into the room. The door slid shut behind him.

Juliet's heart pounded.

In one hand he held a bottle of wine, in the other a velvet box. He set them down on the table nearest the bed, then continued towards her, not stopping until he was close enough so that she could see every nuance of his face and feel the warmth from his body. Much too close.

Her stomach knotted and butterflies seemed to fly up her throat. This was the moment she had been dreading as much as she had been longing for it. He was finally going to consummate their marriage.

'Juliet,' he said softly, taking her hands in his, 'it is time.'

She nodded, allowing him to lead her back to the bed. He released her and poured them each a glass of golden wine. She took hers and sipped. It was champagne. The bubbles floated up her throat. A surprised smile eased some of her discomfort.

He watched her with an intensity that brought back her sense of impending disaster. Intuitively she knew that when he was finished with her nothing would ever be the same. She swallowed down the wine in one long gulp.

He shook his head. 'Fine wine is for sipping, not quenching your thirst.' Still, he poured her more.

This time she sipped, allowing the effervescence to cascade down her throat as she wondered what he was going to do next. Anticipation was a delicious tingle in her toes. None the less, it was a shock when he undid the belt on his robe and allowed the silk to fall to the floor.

He stood naked before her, his magnificent body glowing in the light from the fire. She gaped, taking in his splendour before squeezing her eyes shut. Her cheeks flamed. The empty glass would have fallen from her nerveless fingers if he had not rescued it.

'Get into bed,' he murmured.

Without opening her eyes, she backed away until her knees hit the mattress. His hands gripped her waist and lifted. He held her against him so she could feel his arousal pressing into her. She gasped and put her hands on his shoulders and pressed, trying to put some distance between them.

'Don't,' he ordered. 'This is only the beginning.'

The beginning of the end, she told herself. He

would take her and make her his. She licked her dry lips. He laid her on the bed.

'Here,' he said, handing her another glass of champagne. 'It will help relax you.'

She opened one eye and took the wine. She needed a lot of relaxing. He grinned indulgently at her as she gulped down the contents.

'Remind me not to waste good wine on you again,' he said, taking the empty glass and setting it on the table.

She began to feel a little giddy and drowsy. It would be so nice to sink into the comfort of the feather bed and sleep.

'You cannot go to sleep yet,' he said, untying the sash of her robe. 'I have things to show you.'

It was an effort to open her eyes, but she managed. He loomed over her, his face golden on one side where the firelight hit it. Overwhelming curiosity drew her gaze downward. Dark hairs scattered across his chest, swirling around his nipples. The temptation to touch was great.

'Go ahead,' he murmured, his voice husky. 'Feel me.'

'How did you know?' she asked, her words only slightly slurred.

'Your face. Every thought you have shows on it.'

When she did nothing, he caught one of her hands and placed it on his chest. The invitation was irresistible. With wonder, she explored the textures of his upper body.

His skin was firm, not as soft as hers, but not coarse either. The dark hairs that had beckoned her twined around her fingers, their wiry toughness so much like him. Firm muscles twitched. When she finally found his nipple, it hardened with an alacrity that enthralled her. She swirled her thumb over the nub until he groaned.

'For a beginner you do very well.'

She smiled, hearing the need in his voice. 'I am a fast learner.'

But she knew it was bravado. She had no idea where they were going or how to get there. He was the one who would control their joining.

With infinite skill, he eased the robe off her shoulders. She shivered as the cool air caressed her exposed skin.

'How can you stand being naked?' she asked.

'Anticipation.'

'Ah,' she murmured, memories of his caresses returning. 'I can understand that.'

'Can you? Then help me get your nightrail off.'

That stopped her. 'Can you not do it with me dressed?'

'I could,' he said, leaning down and catching her nipple in his mouth through the fine linen. He sucked and nibbled until she shivered with delight.

He raised his head to watch the wonder moving over her face. 'But it is not nearly so nice.'

'If it were any more so, I would not be able to stand it,' she murmured.

'Oh, you will,' he promised, easing the material over her head.

He dropped the clothing on the floor with his robe, the two garments entwining as he imagined their bodies soon would. His heart hammered with desire. It was all he could do not to enter her now.

She flinched, but did nothing to stop his hand from cupping her breast. His warmth felt good, adding another layer to the sensations he gave her. This time when he took her into his mouth his tongue slid smoothly over her flesh.

'Oh,' she whispered. 'I see what you meant. This is much better.'

He chuckled. For an innocent she was certainly hedonistic. All the better. Her arousal would intensify his reaction.

He reached across her for his half-full glass of champagne. With a tilt of his wrist, he poured some on to her flat abdomen. She flinched, pushing her breasts up against his chest.

'What are you doing?' she asked, raising her head so she could see.

'Patience,' he said, lowering his head to her belly.

With flicks of his tongue he licked up the wine. Her muscles spasmed at each touch.

Juliet had never known such pleasure. She caught his hair in her fingers and held him to her. He chuckled and his warm breath on her skin was like torture. Divine torture that she knew was only the beginning.

Some of the champagne slipped down to the secret place between her legs. He followed it.

Juliet stiffened and tried to pull his head up. 'Please, no.'

He looked up at her, his face implacable. 'Yes.'

She shook her head.

He smiled and slipped his hand where his mouth wanted to go.

She gasped, her eyes wide. 'What are you doing?'

'Making love to you,' he murmured, watching carefully as his fingers slid along the moist warmth of her skin. When he slid one into her, she tightened, and a groan of anticipation escaped him.

Juliet licked dry lips and stared up at the ceiling. She could not watch what he was doing. It was too intimate, too depraved. But it felt so good. She moaned.

'Relax,' he crooned. 'This night is for pleasure.'

Still unable to look at him, she murmured, 'This is so…so unladylike. I never imagined it would be so—'

'Delightful?'

'That too.' She gasped as he found a particularly sensitive spot.

He chuckled, and in her moment of weakness

moved her legs apart and touched her with his tongue. Juliet cringed, only to have shivers rack her body with each caress he gave her. Her stomach clenched.

'What is happening?' she gasped.

He raised up on his elbows to better see her face. 'You are becoming aroused.'

She gulped as his fingers replaced his mouth. 'Oh.'

It was a small sound and all she could make. Her world was spiralling down to the way he made her feel. Nothing else mattered any more. Not the indignity of her position or the crudity of what he was doing. Only the way he made her feel.

Sebastian watched her, his own need mounting. She responded with such sweet intensity he did not know how much longer he could put off entering her completely. He felt her muscles contract and knew she was close.

Never taking his fingers from her, he slid up until he lay in the valley between her legs. Her whimpers drew him on.

In one smooth motion, he pulled out his fingers and inserted himself. He slid in with only a slight hitch.

'Ohh! That hurt.' Her eyes opened and she stared up at him where he lay above her.

He clenched his teeth. 'I…I took your maidenhood.'

She said nothing.

Driven nearly beyond his celebrated control, Sebastian kissed her. He kissed her as if there was no stopping them. Only when she started to kiss him back did he start slowly moving.

She gasped.

He grinned, not knowing it was nearly a grimace. 'Move with me,' he murmured. 'Match my rhythm.'

'I cannot,' she whispered, eyes wide in shock at the knowledge he was inside her. Yet it felt good. Terribly good.

'Yes, you can,' he said, catching her face between his hand and taking her mouth again.

His tongue slipped into her mouth and teased hers. His body slid over hers, his belly meeting hers in shivering pleasure. He moved faster.

Juliet gave in to the demands of his desire. Her hips met his and withdrew in response to his. Her back arched and her breasts pressed tightly against his chest. Sensations drenched her nerves. Her nails raked down his back until her hands clutched his buttocks and urged him on.

Her gasps matched his.

'Now, now,' he moaned.

She thrust up and exploded. Spasms of pleasure tore her apart. She could hardly breathe.

His mouth still covered hers when he lost control. His shout filled her lungs as he bucked into her.

It was a long time before either could move. She

lay beneath him her legs still wrapped around his hips, her eyes slumberous jewels that watched him with satisfaction.

'You are very, very good,' she murmured, running her fingers along his spine. 'I never imagined it could be like that.'

He grinned, enjoying her feather touch on his back. 'Not a fate worse than death after all?'

She smiled and tightened her legs, making him wonder if he would soon be able to repeat what had brought the glow to her body. He certainly wanted to.

Soon he was moving in her again as she moaned and thrashed beneath him. He began to wonder if he would survive the night. If not, he could not think of a better way to end.

Chapter Twelve

Juliet woke up the next day with a sense of well-being. She sighed and tried to roll over. A heavy arm held her pinned to the bed. Soft snores gently blew the curls from her face. Brabourne had stayed the night with her.

She smiled, remembering all they had done to and with each other. Never in her wildest imagination would she have created the things he had done to her. Not even *The Bride of Abydos* had prepared her for the bliss of making love. She flushed as desire quickened her blood.

His eyes opened and she wondered if she had spoken aloud. He gave her a slow, sensual smile, and before she knew it she had straddled him. She lowered herself until he filled her.

'Do your duty, wife,' he said, his voice a hoarse growl.

Feeling her power over him in this position, she

took her time, drawing it out until he begged. When she felt him jerk and his eyes close, she knew he had taken his pleasure.

After his breathing returned to normal, he opened his eyes and said, 'Now it is your turn.'

She squealed as he flipped her over and began doing things to her that she remembered only too well. They had not slept much the night before.

He teased her with mouth, tongue and hands until she was hot and ready. Then he slipped into her.

She watched him with eyes glazed by passion, waiting for him to start the rhythm that ended in such delight. He began slowly so that her tension mounted.

'Brabourne,' she pleaded, her hands on his hips urging him to greater speed.

'Sebastian,' he said.

'Yes, yes,' she muttered. 'Faster, please, I am so—'

'Sebastian.'

She gazed up at him, not knowing what he wanted. She wiggled her hips, hoping to entice him into doing what she needed so desperately.

'Call me Sebastian,' he said, holding back so his face was a grimace caused by the effort it took not to ram into her and take them both to the top.

'Brabourne. Sebastian,' she said, wriggling beneath him. 'They are both your names.'

'Sebastian,' he gritted. 'That is my Christian

name.' He panted as he held back. 'Call me Sebastian and I will end this torture.'

'What's in a name?' she muttered. 'Sebastian.'

He released a pent-up sigh and thrust deep. She arched up to meet him, their bodies straining.

Some time later she woke to find him gone. The bed seemed too large and very cold without him. She rose and wrapped her robe tight before going to the window. Pulling the curtains back, she saw it was dusk. She had spent the entire day in bed. She never did that. But, then, she had never made love to a man all night and day either.

When she finally went downstairs, Burroughs met her in the foyer. 'His Grace is waiting in the library, your Grace.'

She glanced at him to see if he had kept a straight face while sprinkling all those 'Graces' in one sentence. He was the perfect butler, his countenance betraying nothing, not even the ridiculousness of the situation.

'Thank you,' she said, and headed off in the direction he indicated.

She knocked and waited for permission to enter. Once it was given, she opened the door and walked through.

Bra—Sebastian stood by the window looking out, his back to her. He was casually dressed, like a country squire, only on him the simplicity was actually striking. Juliet sighed. He was a magnificent man.

He turned and smiled, the emotion actually reaching his eyes. 'Come here. I want to show you something before it is completely dark.'

She moved to him until they stood side by side. He slipped an arm around her shoulders.

'Look out there,' he directed.

An expanse of grass stretched to the horizon. Every imaginable tree dotted the earth. Manicured gardens of roses, nasturtiums, honeysuckle and much more tempted the beholder to walk through them. A lake in the distance reflected the red rays of the dying sun. Further still were cultivated fields and the smoke from tenants' cottages.

'It is impressive,' she said, not knowing what his point was.

'Yes. And it is mine.' His voice firmed. 'And it will pass to the first male child you bear.'

She stiffened.

He turned her to face him, but she refused to look at him. He caught her chin and made her eyes meet his.

'I know you were a virgin last night, so I know you are not carrying another man's child. Don't betray me as my mother did my father.'

She gazed at the flat blue of his eyes. She now understood that his feelings on this subject were so strong he hid them behind a blank surface. Still, his assumption that she might be unfaithful hurt.

She took a deep breath before speaking. 'I am not your mother. I have already told you I will honour my vows. Obviously you did not believe me.'

He stared down at her, his countenance still inscrutable. 'Ours was not a love match—I don't expect fidelity. Just wait until after I have an heir.'

She slapped him, her reaction instinctual. 'How dare you accuse me of your sins? When I said I honour my vows, I meant I honour them for my lifetime.'

She wrenched from his loosened embrace and stormed to the door and through it.

Sebastian watched her go before turning back to the view. He was sorry to have hurt her, but she had to understand. He would not brook raising another man's bastard as his heir. He would divorce her and disown the child first.

Still, he wished it could have been different. A part of him wished he could have trusted her. But trust was something he had never learned to have for women.

That night he came to her and she let him make love to her, knowing he would visit her every night until she conceived his heir. It was bitter-sweet knowledge as she dissolved under his caresses.

* * *

The next morning Juliet woke to an empty bed, the warmth and intimacy of their first night together gone. The loss brought tears she could not stem. For a while she had allowed herself to enjoy her husband's attentions without feeling the future press down on her.

The door between hers and Sebastian's rooms opened. He entered, dressed for riding.

'I am touring the estate today. Would you like to come along?'

'Why?' she asked without thinking, concerned only with concealing the fact that she had been crying. She swiped at her cheeks.

He flinched before his cool hauteur returned. 'I deserved that. I would like to show you around and introduce you to some of the people. This is your home now, and will be so for the children you bear.'

Her stomach churned. The children she bore, not *their* children. 'Any children I have will belong here.'

He nodded. 'Are you coming?'

He was implacable. She was tempted to throw his invitation back in his face, but she was also curious. As he had pointed out, she would spend a large part of her life here.

'Give me a few minutes to dress.'

'I will be in the library.'

She made a fast toilet and descended the stairs in her leaf-green riding habit. A jaunty black hat with a lone peacock feather tilted rakishly on her auburn curls. She looked her best and knew it. Somehow she did not think it would make any difference. Sebastian had his pick of beautiful women and trusted none of them. Beauty would not win him, but it gave her courage to know he would not be embarrassed to introduce her as his Duchess.

They wasted no time.

Juliet rode a placid gelding while Sebastian rode a spirited mare. He led the way down a dirt road.

Rich fields spread out around them. She could see people working the earth. Up ahead was a cottage with a woman and child standing outside.

Sebastian reined in. 'How are you, Mrs Smith?'

The woman bobbed a curtsy. 'Well, your Grace. The harvest will be large this year.'

'We can use it,' Sebastian said. 'I have brought my bride. You will be seeing a lot of her.'

The woman made another curtsy. 'Your Grace.'

Juliet smiled. 'How old is your child and what is his name?'

'He be eight. We call him Tom after his pa.'

Juliet smiled at the boy who stood bravely beside his mother, taking in the novelty of the lord and lady speaking with them. He raised his hand to a lock of hair and tugged it.

'We must be going,' Sebastian said. 'Let my steward know if there is anything you need.'

At the next house a young girl met them. She bobbed respectfully. 'Your Grace.'

Sebastian nodded and introduced Juliet. After the acknowledgments, he asked, 'Where are your parents?'

'In the village getting provisions.'

'Tell them someone will be out within the week with materials to repair your roof.' And they were off again.

By the end of the afternoon Juliet felt as though she had met more people in the past few hours than in the last year. All of them were well fed and seemed contented. Sebastian was a good landlord. She was not surprised.

That night she fell into bed, tired and aching. It had been a while since she had spent so much time in the saddle. Not even a hot bath had helped. Her eyes were drowsily shutting when the door opened. She suppressed a groan of pure exhaustion.

Without asking permission, Sebastian got under the covers of her bed and snuffed the candle he carried and set it on the table. He reached for her.

Juliet scooted back. 'Please, not tonight. I ache in all the wrong places.'

'Ah. Too long on horseback.'

She rolled over on her back. 'Yes. I have not ridden like that since before Mama died. Coupled with the soreness from our activities, I feel I am splitting apart.'

He chuckled. 'Poor Juliet. Come here and let me rub your back and legs.'

She snorted. 'I know where that will lead.'

'I promise.'

She knew he would keep a promise. And it did sound divine.

'Just for a little bit.'

'Of course,' he murmured.

She rolled onto her stomach and let him do as he would. His fingers dug into the sore muscles of her lower back and thighs. At first it hurt, but soon she loosened as his massage continued. Shortly she purred contentment.

'Glad now?' he asked, his voice husky as his fingers moved down from the small of her back.

Little jolts of pleasure shot through her as he rubbed. 'You are very good,' she murmured.

Instead of answering, he turned her on her side and cuddled her close. 'I will leave you alone tonight,' he said, wrapping his arm around her waist so that his hand cupped her breast.

'You have a very unusual way of doing that,' she muttered, wiggling into him.

'And you have a very tempting way of getting comfortable.'

She stopped all movement. As much as she enjoyed his lovemaking, she was truly sore and tired. With a sigh she closed her eyes and tried not to let hope flare in her heart. He was staying only because he was determined she would have *his* child. Sadness filled her instead as she drifted to sleep.

The next morning Juliet drifted awake, feeling warm and cosy. She snuggled into the source of her delight.

'Time to wake up,' Sebastian murmured, his lips skimming along her face.

She opened her eyes and looked straight into his. Their blue depths were filled with desire and she knew there would be no denying him this time. Nor did she want to.

Two days later, she sat in the Duke of Brabourne's travelling carriage, the Brabourne crest emblazoned on the glossy black paint outside. The thick gold velvet seats were the most comfortable she had ever ridden in. Sebastian rode his favourite horse.

Brabourne Abbey disappeared from sight and Juliet leaned back into the cushions. They were going to London. She had not wanted to leave, thinking that with time and no other distractions she might win her husband's trust, if not his love. He had not given her that time.

She sighed and forced herself to read the book she had brought along. The journey would be too short.

* * *

Juliet could have done without dinner at Carlton House, but Brabourne—no, Sebastian—was still one of Prinny's intimates regardless of being married now. She supposed she should consider herself lucky she had also been invited.

Resigned, she took another bite of salmon and smiled at her dinner partner, Lord Appleby. He was tall and slim, an elegant man with blond hair and a dimple when he smiled. He was also a witty talker and a wicked flirt. Innuendoes fell from his lips like water from an icicle.

Sebastian was further up the table near Prinny. So was her stepmother, but that did not bother her much. What ate at her was the woman beside her husband. She was beautiful and endowed in ways Juliet never would be. She also constantly touched Sebastian, and he enjoyed it if his sultry smile was anything to go by. Watching them was like twisting a knife in her heart. If she could, she would leave. She could not.

She took another bite and looked away. There was nothing she could do, no matter how much it hurt. She would worry about something else, such as the way Papa was watching Emily flirt with the Prince. He had the same gleam in his eye that had been there the night she had overheard him tell Hobson about challenging Sebastian. He absolutely could not challenge the Prince. That was treason.

'Lady Brabourne,' Lord Appleby said, breaking

into her thoughts, 'you have not heard a word I have been saying and now dinner is over. You owe me the pleasure of your company for a walk.'

She turned and blinked at him. She owed him? She pulled herself together and glanced at her husband, only to see him still flirting with the same woman. Perhaps she did owe Appleby after all. He rose and she allowed him to take her hand.

Sebastian watched his bride walk off with one of the most notorious womanisers in London. Michael Appleby had been chasing skirts since their days at Eton. Appleby left his own wife in the country while he pursued his pleasures in town.

A spurt of anger caught Sebastian unawares. He did not want Juliet consorting with the likes of Appleby, not after all he had done to improve her reputation. With a murmured excuse, he extricated himself from his companion's clutches.

The couple sauntered ahead. Sebastian knew exactly where their roundabout walk was taking them. He had entertained his share of women there, too.

Juliet allowed Appleby to guide her down ornately decorated halls where footmen stood around doing nothing. All the while he kept up a witty monologue. He stopped at a door that was indistinguishable from the others, but he seemed to know where they were.

Smiling down at her, he said, 'There is an Italian picture in here that I would like your opinion on.'

She studied him in the light provided by wall sconces. His hazel eyes dared her, and his dimple teased her. She wondered how many women he had charmed with those two assets.

'An Italian picture?' She grinned at him. She was married to Brabourne and knew what a rake looked like when he was bent on conquest. 'That sounds perilously close to a walk in a darkened garden.'

His smile widened. 'You are too astute for me. Brabourne must have taught you well.'

She shrugged. The last thing she intended to discuss was her husband.

With a mock sigh, he extended his arm once more. 'Let me escort you back to the salon.'

'That will not be necessary,' Sebastian said, coming round the corner where he had stopped to see what Juliet would do.

Appleby frowned before stepping away graciously. 'Over-protective, ain't you?'

Sebastian gave him a feral parting of lips. 'I know you too well, my friend.'

Appleby's gaze went from Sebastian to Juliet and back. 'I once thought the same of you. But things seem to have changed.'

'Precisely.'

Juliet watched the two men and wondered what they were really saying to each other. With a mock bow, Appleby sauntered off. Sebastian turned his attention to her.

'What was that all about?' she asked. When he did not answer, she narrowed her eyes. 'Don't look at me like that. I did not do anything wrong.'

'I know,' he said solemnly. 'But you need to know I am not my father, my dear. I will not share.'

She clenched her teeth and glared at him. 'Neither will I. So you had better remember that!'

The corner of his mouth twitched. 'What is good for the goose is good for the gander?'

'Absolutely,' she huffed.

Head high, she skirted past him, resisting the urge to stay close. It was a battle she fought every time he was near. But this time she was not going to weaken. How dared he tell her to be faithful when he was not? And then to be amused when she told him he had to be equally true to her. More amazing than anything was that she had told him anything. He was not a man one gave ultimatums to, and she had told herself she would never do so. She would do her best to accept his infidelities.

She shook her head at her bravado. A giggle of nervous reaction bubbled to her lips which she smothered with a hand.

She rounded a corner well ahead of Sebastian and came to a dead halt. Down the long hall, in plain sight for anyone to see, the Prince stood kissing and embracing her stepmother. All thought of her bold words to Sebastian evaporated in the anger that gripped her. Her hands fisted. More than anything she wanted to hurt Emily. How dared she do this to Papa?

'I would be careful about what I do. Attacking the Prince could be construed as treason,' Sebastian said in a sardonic whisper.

Juliet shot him a fulminating glance. Keeping her voice as low as his, she hissed, 'It is Emily I wish to kill.'

Sebastian took her arm and steered her back around the corner and out of sight, shaking his head the entire time. 'I shall be careful not to anger you for I am looking forward to a long life.'

He was teasing her, and at a time like this. She rounded on him, hands on hips. 'This is awful. What will Papa say if he finds out? It will break his heart.'

Sebastian moved his hands to her shoulders and scowled. 'You cannot protect him from everything. You certainly cannot fight a duel with Prinny. It isn't done.'

'Then what am I supposed to do? Stand by and let that…that *woman* hurt Papa? I do not think so.'

He shook her. 'Don't be ridiculous. Your father is a grown man. He can and should take care of his own problems.'

Her face scrunched up and it was all she could do not to shout in her frustration. 'I promised Mama. I have to take care of him.'

'No, you don't, Juliet. What she made you promise was unfair. You were hurting and under duress. You must let it go.'

She twisted in his hold, but he tightened his grip. Part of her knew he was right, but a larger part could not release her from her promise. Not yet.

'Remove your hands, please,' she said hoarsely. 'I need to find Papa and make sure he does not come this way.'

Sebastian did as she asked, but stayed close, blocking her from an easy exit. 'You are the most stubborn woman it has ever been my misfortune to meet. Your father is a grown man. Let him solve his own problems, especially since he seems to make all of them. No other man in his right mind would have married Emily Winters. Forget the past.'

She lashed out at him. 'Then what about you? Instead of carrying your hatred of your mother around like a mountain on your shoulder, why don't you forget? Do as you order me to do.'

He stepped away and all emotion fled from his face. 'You hit below the belt, madam.'

'So do you,' she muttered.

Not meeting his burning gaze, she started edging around him. Fortunately, the walls were as wide as they were opulently decorated. The Prince Regent skimped on nothing. She looked up just in time to see Papa rounding the nearest corner. She groaned.

Sebastian heard her and pivoted to find out what

was the matter. He put a hand on Juliet's arm.
'Don't interfere.'

Ignoring him, she stepped in front of her parent.
'Papa, are you lost? Let me show you the way back
to the drawing room.'

He did not even glance at her, only swerved to
miss her and continued down the hallway. She
shook off Sebastian's hand and ran after him. Papa
turned the corner and halted so quickly the tails of
his coat were still visible to her. She reached him
and wrapped both hands around his right arm.

'I am sure there is a reason for this,' she spouted,
without thinking how inane her words sounded.

He stared at his Prince and his wife. As though
sensing they were no longer alone, the couple slowly
separated and looked towards where Juliet and her
father stood. The Prince had the grace to flush, the
colour heightened by his ruddy complexion. Emily
gasped and moved further away from her royal conquest.

Juliet dug her nails deeper into Papa's arm. He
seemed impervious to anything she did or said, his
focus completely on the couple.

'You cannot challenge *him* to a duel,' a dry voice
said. 'It's considered treason.'

Juliet breathed a sigh of relief. Even though she
knew Sebastian would not interfere, having him
close gave her a sense of strength. If nothing else,
he might keep Papa from doing something rash.

'Just showing Lady Smythe-Clyde around,' the Prince said, moving away from Emily as he walked towards the trio.

Emily loosed her tinkling laugh. For the first time since Juliet had met the woman, the noise sounded strained.

'Oliver, darling, Prinny has been so kind as to point out his works of art to me and tell me where they are from.' She stopped by her husband and linked her arm in his.

Juliet watched everything, eyes wide, ready to jump between everyone if that seemed necessary. Sebastian's light touch at her waist would not stop her.

Lord Smythe-Clyde stared down at his wife for a long time. His jaw worked and the hand of his free arm clenched and unclenched. Juliet held her breath.

With no warning, her father gave the Prince a curt bow. 'Your Highness, we must leave.' Nor did he wait for permission. He moved off so quickly that Emily stumbled and would have fallen if Smythe-Clyde had not had a death grip on her arm.

Juliet released her pent-up breath, nearly sagging in the process. Sebastian's arm slid completely around her waist and held her. His solid strength and warmth felt good.

Sebastian shook his head. 'That was not well done, my liege. You know Smythe-Clyde's propensity for violent retribution.'

Prinny shuddered. 'Yes, but he could not challenge me.' He watched until the other couple were gone from sight. 'I almost feel sorry for her.'

'I don't,' Juliet retorted. 'She needs a comeuppance.' She gave the Prince a jaundiced look that said she thought he did as well. Once more he flushed.

'Well, I must be getting back to my other guests,' he blustered.

After sufficient time had passed, Sebastian turned Juliet in the circle of his arms so that she faced him. 'That was not so hard, was it?'

After a second's resistance, she allowed herself to sink into the comfort of his strength. Now that the crisis was past, she began to shake. He held her closer. When the short reaction had run its course, she pushed away from him. He let her move several inches so they could see each other's face.

'It was certainly not easy. I thought for a moment Papa would either challenge him or hit him.'

She closed her eyes on the picture of mayhem that would have ensued. Sebastian's lips on her forehead brought her back.

'He handled it on his own. I doubt Emily will be quite so free with her favours in the future.'

'Papa has never done that before,' she said in wonder.

He raised one brow. 'I doubt you or your mother ever let him before.'

He had a point, and rather than argue she said, 'We must return or people will begin to wonder.'

The slow, sensual smile that made her stomach flutter parted his lips. She gulped, but could not look away from the deep blue of his eyes.

'Let them. We are married. Remember?'

His voice was deep and caught on the last word. She knew what that meant.

'We cannot,' she said, panic rising. 'We are not at home.'

His smile turned sardonic. 'There are plenty of places here, believe me.'

Pain flared, squeezing her chest, at this reminder of how experienced he was. She twisted in his arms. 'Thank you, but I don't wish to have that experience.'

His grip tightened. One hand caught her jaw and forced her to meet his gaze. 'Juliet, I have been a rake. You knew that when we wed. Nothing can ever change that.'

'Yes,' she whispered. 'That is why I did not want to marry you.'

His eyes darkened as though she had hurt him. 'But because of that I am skilled and you enjoy my lovemaking.' Memory lit fires in his body. 'You like it a lot.'

She closed her eyes, not wanting to see the hunger in his, not wanting to be drawn into the passion he did nothing to control. 'Yes, but not here. Please.'

It was an eternity before he released her. She had begun to despair that he would listen to her plea. With cold formality, he offered his arm. With the best face she could summon, she laid her fingers on his coat, barely touching him.

That night he came to her bed and made fierce love to her as though demons drove him. She lost herself in his passion and was glad for it. Nothing else mattered.

Chapter Thirteen

Juliet laughed from sheer pleasure. The veil of her riding hat billowed out behind her as her mare flew along the bridle path in Green Park. She heard the pounding hooves of Sebastian's gelding gaining on her. She urged her mount on.

Out of the corner of her eye, she saw Sebastian's horse edge closer until it was even with her. Sebastian reached out and grabbed her mare's bridle. Juliet grinned at him.

Rather than risk either of them or their horses being hurt when it was not necessary, she pulled in on the reins. Her mare slowed until she walked. Sebastian did the same. They continued to walk their horses while the animals cooled down.

After a time, they meandered to the early-morning shade provided by a huge oak tree. Sebastian dismounted, then went to Juliet and grabbed her waist.

She put her hands on his shoulders and slid down the length of him. Excitement curled in her stomach.

He held her a long time.

'Why are you staring?' she asked, her brows furrowed. 'You have seen me look a mess before.'

He tucked several tendrils of hair behind her ear, a gesture she had come to expect from him when she was dishevelled. Then he righted her riding hat so that it sat at an angle on her head and the ostrich feathers tickled her cheek.

'You are so vibrant,' he said. 'I have never met a woman before with your enthusiasm for life, and not just in bed.'

This was so unlike him that she became embarrassed. 'I am sure you exaggerate.'

'No.' He abruptly released her and turned away.

She reached for him, wanting the security of feeling his body. Something was very wrong this morning. He did not draw away from her touch, but neither did he cup his hand over hers as he usually did.

'What is the matter?'

'Nothing,' he said curtly. Before she could remonstrate with him, he asked, 'Do you recognise this tree?'

Nonplussed, she stepped back and looked at the tree. It was obvious Sebastian was not going to tell her what troubled him. Absent-mindedly she studied the oak. Then it came to her.

'This is where we duelled. It seems like an eternity ago.'

He nodded, his mouth curling sardonically. 'It certainly seems that. So many things in our lives were changed by that one act.'

Dismay swamped her. She knew he would not have married her without being forced, but she had fooled herself into thinking he was at least contented with their union. He definitely seemed that way in bed. But then he was a man and a rake. Lovemaking was his forte. All the pleasure of the morning and the ride evaporated. She wanted to go home.

'We should be leaving. There are so many things to do today. I have to return Maria Sefton's visit, and I must write to Papa.' Sebastian raised an eyebrow in disbelief. 'I know he very likely does not read my letters, but it gives me comfort to tell him how things are going in London. Since he forced Emily to return to the country, I find I miss them. Silly, but Papa has always been a large part of my life.'

She stopped. She was rambling on in an attempt to cover the hurt his mood had brought on. Better to be quiet.

'Thank goodness they are gone, and good riddance. Heaven only knows what you would have done next in your misguided efforts to protect him from the world. I don't like to think of it.'

She hoped he was trying to be amusing, but there

was no glint of humour in his eyes. He was deadly serious. The knowledge added to her discomfort. Just a week ago she would have argued with him, but not now. Not here.

'Please help me to mount. If we don't get home soon, I shall not have time to change for my visit.'

He did so and they cantered home, neither saying anything.

At the townhouse a groom helped Juliet dismount. She thanked him and went inside. She smiled at Burroughs and a nearby footman. Burroughs gave her a disapproving look while the footman smiled shyly.

'Your Grace,' the butler said, taking her riding crop. 'I hope you enjoyed yourself.'

'Oh, yes. Since we returned to London I have missed riding more than anything.'

'You ride,' Sebastian said, entering behind her and handing Burroughs his hat and crop.

'In Rotten Row,' she said derisively. 'That is meandering.'

He flicked her cheek. 'I must finish some work. I will see you later.'

She watched him go, wondering how long she would be able to stand the sham of their marriage. She knew everyone married for convenience, as had they, but her feelings had gone beyond that. She loved him.

Sebastian went up the stairs and she watched him

avidly. She wanted so much for him to love her as well as desire her. It was an ache in her heart.

'Ahem.' Burroughs interrupted her thoughts. 'Mrs Burroughs has the week's menus ready when you have time, your Grace.'

'Thank you. I will meet with her later.'

Burroughs bowed and left to perform his other duties.

Juliet turned to see if any notes, invitations or messages were on the silver tray by the door.

Only one envelope lay on the salver. There was no visible writing so she picked it up and turned it over. An overly ornate feminine hand had written 'Sebastian'. That was all, except for the heavy scent of tuberose.

Juliet licked suddenly dry lips. Her hand began to shake so that it was a supreme effort to return the note to the tray without dropping it. She stared at nothing, wondering why having the truth staring her in the face was so much worse than just thinking about it. Sebastian had never promised to be faithful.

'Your Grace?' Burroughs asked, louder than normal.

'Yes,' she said, her voice a croak.

'Are you all right? Should I send a footman for the doctor?'

He must have returned while she stood numbly. She turned to him, still dazed from the heartache eating away at her chest. 'A doctor?' Could a doctor mend a broken heart? She was ready to cry. 'No, thank you.'

Before he could ask something else, she walked past him towards the back of the house and went out into the garden. She needed to be alone. She had Sebastian's name and as much of his lovemaking as any woman could want. They were not enough. She wanted his love.

She wandered down the path leading to a white gazebo where roses climbed towards the sun. The peace and scent of fresh roses always made her feel better. Perhaps they would help. She sank on to her favourite bench and cupped a blossom in her palm, inhaled the wonderful fragrance. It was lovely, but, as she had known, it was not enough. Nothing would ever be enough to dull the pain of her husband's infidelities. Nothing.

Hands clasped in her lap, she closed her eyes and let the tears fall.

Sebastian found her half an hour later, his forehead creased in worry. Burroughs had come to his rooms and told him her Grace was not feeling well. From the butler's tone, Sebastian knew he wondered if Juliet was pregnant. Sebastian wondered himself. Part of him hoped so.

She looked pale and tired. He should not have talked to her this morning the way he had, but he had not known exactly what was happening to him.

He still did not know. The oak tree had brought back the memory of their duel and for an instant he had been glad she had fought it. Which was preposterous. She had entered his life and nothing was the same. He did not even visit his former lady-friends.

He sat beside her and took her hand. 'Are you sick? Is your shoulder still paining you?'

She opened her eyes and looked at him. Their green depths sparkled with unshed tears. 'No, I am fine.'

He traced the path of one tear with his finger. 'Then why have you been crying?'

She turned away and her voice came out barely audible. 'I am tired, that is all.'

'Are you in the family way?' He caught her chin and gently drew her face back so he could watch for her reaction.

She shook her head. 'No. I don't think so.'

'Ah.' Disappointment he had not thought he would experience shafted through him. There is plenty of time for that, he told himself. 'Then it must be too many late nights and too much of your husband's attentions,' he added with a lecherous smile.

She gazed dully at him. 'Perhaps. I think I should lie down.' She stood and looked down at him. 'Alone.'

He rose and took one of her hands in his. 'Are you sure?'

'Yes.'

He released her and stepped away. He had seen people look as she did, usually when they had lost everything. It made no sense for her to feel that way. He had given her their world.

Maybe questioning Burroughs more thoroughly would bring something to light.

That night at dinner she looked no better for her rest. Sebastian watched her pick at her food, moving it around on her plate and cutting it into small pieces she did not eat. Nor did she drink any wine.

She looked up from her activity and caught him watching her. The circles under her eyes accentuated her high cheekbones. 'Will you be staying in to-night?'

She had never asked him that before. He pondered her question before answering. Did she know about his summons and who it was from? He did not think so.

'No. I am to meet Ravensford and Perth at White's,' he lied with smooth proficiency.

'I see,' she mumbled. 'If you will excuse me?' She pushed back her chair before the footman could help and left the room without glancing back.

Sebastian rose, his only thought to follow and comfort her. He got three steps and stopped. This was not the time. Something was upsetting her and he could not spare the time to find out what.

His mother waited.

*   *   *

Juliet pulled the hood of her black cape more securely around her face. Her fingers clenched the heavy wool so tightly her nails went through, and she had to blink rapidly to rid her eyes of the moisture blurring her vision. Ahead of her, Sebastian moved quickly through the early evening shadows. He was going to another woman.

Thankful it was dusk and the shadows were settling, she edged into the doorway of a closed shop. A few people still milled around, some with purpose, others aimlessly. They helped keep her hidden as well. Not that Sebastian would look. He thought she was safely at home reading a book while he cavorted.

She knew she was making a mistake. A wife did not follow her husband to his mistress's abode. It was very improper. It also hurt as nothing else she had ever experienced—except, perhaps, finding out about the infidelity.

He was heading towards Piccadilly. She hastened to keep up, his height the only thing that allowed her to keep him in sight. Without once looking back or around, so she knew that he did not know she was following him, he entered the Pulteney. It was where the Tsar and his sister had stayed when they'd visited London in 1814.

She was surprised. She had thought his mistress would be set up in a house somewhere. Still, if she was a member of Society, she might meet him here.

However blasé her husband might be, he would not want his wife meeting another man in their own home. Even Juliet understood that much about dalliances.

She could not follow him into the hotel without drawing attention she did not want. No one must know what she was doing. With a sigh, she settled into a shadowed alcove across the street to wait, thankful she had remembered to bring the little one-shot pistol Harry had given her a number of years before. No matter how decent an area might be, a woman alone was at risk. She had learned that lesson well in Vauxhall.

Sebastian strode through the lobby of the Pulteney towards the stairs and the room the note had indicated. This was the last place he wanted to be. His jaw twitched and the tic at his right eye was a constant irritant. But he had no choice.

Reaching the door, he stood and did nothing. Many years had passed since he had last seen his mother. He did not want to see her now, but neither did he want her setting up house in England. He had given her plenty of money to move to Italy. He still gave her a very generous quarterly allowance.

Girding himself for the encounter, he knocked sharply. Her imperious 'Come in' filtered through the door, making her voice soft like a young girl's. Sebastian grimaced and entered.

She sat straight-backed in a chair pulled close to the fire. Her once-black hair was streaked with silver. It was the most obvious change in her.

'Have a seat,' she said, motioning with her hand to another chair. 'I have much to say to you and would prefer not to look up. It puts a crick in my neck that later gives me a headache.'

That was just like her, Sebastian thought, doing as she said. Even knowing it was crazy, he acknowledged that his mother had a hold over him. First it had been the love of a child for the parent. Later it had been disgust at her stream of lovers, and later than that it had been hatred when he had learned he was not the son of the Duke of Brabourne. Her hold on him now was curiosity. He needed to learn why she had returned and speed her removal back to Italy, preferably without her meeting Juliet.

'Would you care for some wine?' she asked.

'No, thank you.'

He crossed one booted leg over the opposite thigh and studied her. In spite of the greying hair, she had aged well. There were lines around her blue eyes and crinkles near her mouth but her skin was still a creamy white with no age spots. Her bearing was regal and her figure slim. She wore a very stylish gown, its simplicity drawing attention to her magnificent bosom and small waist. A multiple strand choker of pearls circled her neck; he assumed it was to hide the wrinkles that were inevitable on that part of the body. Her vanity would make that a necessity.

'Why have you come back?' he asked, determined to finish this quickly.

'You always were brash and disrespectful.'

'Not always,' he murmured.

She cocked her head to one side. 'No, I suppose not. When you were young you were loving and eager to do anything asked of you. You changed.'

He was surprised to hear regret in her words. He had not thought her capable of anything but self-interest. 'I changed because of what you did.'

She sighed and her gaze dropped to her folded hands. Her black lashes hid any emotion that might show in her eyes. 'I did what was necessary. I am sorry if it hurt you.'

A sharp bark of laughter escaped the tightness in his throat. 'Sorry? You should have thought of that while you were busy sleeping with every man in England.'

Her laugh was bitter. 'I was not talking about that. I meant marrying Brabourne, even though he was not your father.'

'You married him while you were carrying me? Did he know it?'

'No,' she murmured. 'I told him you were early. At first he believed me, but the nurses talked and he heard them. They said you were too big for a premature baby.'

'Why did you do it?' He could barely believe what she was saying. Not only was the man he had considered his father for years not, but he had been tricked into marrying a woman he did not know was pregnant.

She twisted a large pearl and diamond ring she wore on her wedding finger. As soon as the late Duke had passed on, she had returned the heirloom engagement ring Juliet now wore. Sebastian had not had to ask for it back.

'It was the only way. I would have been ostracised. You would have been a bastard. I could not let any of that happen.' For the first time since they had started talking she sounded anxious.

He stared at her. 'You tricked him. The least you could have done was tell him and let him make the choice.'

She shook her head. 'No. He would not have married me. He was a proud man. Much as you are. I could not have had you out of wedlock. I could not do that to you or myself.'

She was right. He would never marry a woman who carried another man's child, no matter what the circumstances. Except…perhaps Juliet. No, he quickly told himself. Not even Juliet.

'What about my real father? Why didn't he marry you?'

She looked back up at him and he thought he saw moisture in her eyes. He had to be mistaken. Never in his entire time with her had he seen her display this much emotion. He did not expect it now.

'He was already married. He said he would leave her and we would go to the Continent. I loved him. I believed him.' She sighed sadly. 'I was a fool.'

Appalled, Sebastian sat like a statue. 'But the other men?'

'You have never been in a loveless relationship. I did not love Brabourne and he never loved me. Ours was a marriage of convenience. Once he realised you were not his, he did not even maintain a semblance of civility to me. He insulted me in front of everyone—our friends and family and the servants. He made my life a living hell.' Anger sparked from her eyes, making her resemble her old self for the first time since her confession had started. 'I hated him, and openly sleeping with other men was the only way I could hurt him. His pride and arrogance could not withstand the public humiliation.'

Sebastian felt the first glimmer of sympathy for her, this woman he had hated all of his adult life. As a child he had not been in his parents' company much, which was normal for the nobility. He had known there was something uncomfortable between them, but he had never understood exactly what it was. Then he had learned of his own background and of his mother's infidelities. After that, nothing had been able to penetrate the wall he put around himself for protection from emotional pain.

'Is this why you came back, to tell me these things?'

She nodded. 'When I heard you were married I felt you needed to know the truth behind my actions. I have always known you hated me. I did not want you to take that hate out on your wife, who is innocent of anything I did.'

Nobility of character in a woman he had always considered to have none—it tugged at the part of him that worried about honour.

It was hard, but he finally managed to say, 'Thank you. I know this could not have been easy.'

She gave him a weak smile. 'No, but I had to do it. I owed you that much. If you hold your wife at arm's length because of what I did, you will forge yourself a miserable life. Even if you did not marry for love, marriage can give you children to love and raise together and bring companionship for your older years.'

For the first time he realised how lonely she must be, exiled to Italy and away from her family. He had not thought of it before, and if he had, he would not have cared. Now it mattered.

He stood and paced the floor, unsure of what he was going to say and how to say it. But he felt impelled to do something. Juliet would certainly expect it of him if she knew about this. He found he expected it of himself.

He stopped and made a conscious effort to ease

the knotting of his shoulder muscles. 'I think my wife would like to meet you. If you have the time.'

She looked up at him and the tears he had imagined before became real. 'I would like that very much.'

Sebastian had never felt so awkward in his life. It was not a pleasant experience. 'Then I will send my carriage round for you tomorrow,' he said gruffly. 'Now I must take my leave and let Juliet know to expect you.'

'Of course,' she said, some of her earlier strength returning. 'Until tomorrow.'

She held out her hand, which he took. He raised it to his lips and brushed her knuckles with his mouth. With her, kissing her fingers was an old-fashioned, courtly action, a gesture from her youth.

He took his leave, wondering where all this would end. The things she had told him eased some of the old hatred, but anger still lingered in the back of his mind. There was too much hurt and not enough time to resolve it. Not yet.

As to how it related to his marriage, he just did not know. Trusting was not easy for him. Trusting a woman was the hardest of all.

Juliet saw him exit the Pulteney. He had been there barely thirty minutes. She knew from their own lovemaking that half an hour was not nearly enough for Sebastian. At least not with her.

Hope rose. Perhaps she had been mistaken. But who could have sent the note and when would he meet with her?

He headed back the way he had come.

It was starting to rain. She huddled into her cape and glanced around, looking for a way to watch him and still keep out of the wet. With a sigh of regret she realised there was no way to avoid the moisture. She would be as soaked as he by the time they got home.

One more look around and she started out.

Something moved in her peripheral vision. A man dressed in black moved along the side of the buildings. If she did not know better, she would think he followed Sebastian. Still, she watched the dark figure for a while. There was something elusively familiar about the way he walked and the tilt of his head. She did not know what exactly, but it was there, teasing at her memory.

A hint of something wrong made her follow behind him as he kept some distance from Sebastian. She edged closer to the man.

'Brabourne,' the man said, his voice carrying in the damp night.

Sebastian turned to see a pistol aimed at his heart. His pulse speeded up and his senses sharpened. This was not the time for him to die. He had too much to do and all of it centred around Juliet.

'Ah, it is you,' he drawled, hoping to keep the

man off guard. 'I see your cheek has healed nicely. The scar becomes you.'

The thug from Vauxhall stepped closer, his face a furious mask. 'You will not be so smug when I have finished with you.'

Under the guise of a bored yawn, Sebastian looked around for some means of distraction. All he needed was to divert the man's attention for a moment. The figure sneaking up on them would do. He was sorry to draw the other person in, but he did not think the thug had the skills to kill both of them. With luck, no one would even be hurt except the would-be killer.

'Don't look now,' Sebastian said drily, 'but there is someone behind you.'

'I don't believe you,' the other growled.

Sebastian shrugged. 'It is your party.'

Doubt flitted across the other man's face, which was a pale oval in the light from a street flambeau. Though not many people were around, this part of Piccadilly was well lit. Soon, however, the light would be gutted by the water coming down.

The rain had soaked Sebastian's hair and made his greatcoat heavy. The man holding him up looked worse, as though he had been waiting in the wet for some time. Sebastian hoped the thug would slip on the cobbles.

The man edged around, keeping the pistol aimed at Sebastian but looking over his shoulder to see if

Sebastian spoke the truth. The figure that had been following them stopped. For the first time Sebastian saw that the innocent he had dragged into this wore a cape. A woman.

'Blast,' he cursed, lunging forward. He could not put a female in danger. No matter what.

He heard a bang and saw a flash of light from the barrel pointed his way. He jerked his torso around so that the ball entered his shoulder instead of the centre of his chest. Pain raked through him.

Another shot rang out.

The figure in front of Sebastian bucked just as Sebastian tackled him. Ignoring the fire radiating out from his shoulder, Sebastian straddled the thug and punched his jaw. The man's head jerked.

'Sebastian. Sebastian, is that you? Are you all right?'

Sebastian could not believe his ears. His head came up just as he landed the thug another facer. 'Juliet? What in blazes are you doing here?'

She fell to her knees beside him. 'I…oh, I cannot tell you. But I am so glad I did. This villain has been following you.'

'Ah, yes.' Sebastian looked down at the man he still straddled. Blood flowed freely from a wound on the thug's right side, soaking through his coat. 'I think he is completely incapacitated.'

'Will he die?' Juliet asked. 'He deserves to, for that is what he intended to happen to you.'

'You are the most bloodthirsty woman I have ever met,' he said, catching the back of her head with one hand and pulling her to him for a long, hungry kiss. 'But I am glad to see you. I think he might have killed me otherwise, instead of just injuring me.'

She blinked water from her eyes. 'Injured! Where? We must get you home. You will catch an inflammation out here.'

He smiled at her, feeling his energy of minutes before seeping out. 'First we must take care of this fellow.'

'Leave him for the night watch, Sebastian. You are more important.'

He staggered to his feet and offered her a hand. She took it and he pulled her up. 'Remind me not to anger you.'

She glared at him. 'Your levity is out of place.'

Ignoring her, he pulled out his handkerchief from inside his coat and wadded it into a ball. With a grimace, he pushed it inside his clothing and pressed it hard to his wound. It was not much, but it was the best he could do under the circumstances.

His teeth started chattering and he noticed her lips were blue. Both of them needed a warm fire and a hot drink, but first he had to take care of this villain. For good this time.

'Juliet, go to the Pulteney and tell them to send

out several servants to help us. I do not intend for this scum to get away.'

She clamped her mouth shut on what he was sure was another reprimand. With a sweep of her soaked cape, she stalked off. His wife had more spirit and courage than ten men. But why had she been following him, for that was the only explanation for her presence? He would find out soon enough.

Chapter Fourteen

Sebastian relaxed into the chair, grateful for the warmth of the nearby fire. A tumbler of whisky and a full decanter sat on the table beside him. The doctor had just left. He had a flesh wound, more painful than serious.

They had taken care of the scoundrel who had shot him and come straight home. Juliet fussed around him, plumping the pillows on the bed and getting his robe.

'You must be cold with just your breeches on,' she said, bringing the fine woollen garment to him.

He leaned forward and allowed her to wrap it around his shoulders. She was careful not to touch his bandage.

'Thank you.' He took a big swallow of whisky, enjoying the warm sensation all the way down his throat. 'Why did you follow me?'

'Why did you go there when you were supposed

to be with Perth and Ravensford?' she countered, meeting his gaze without any hint of remorse.

He swirled the burnt brown liquid and sniffed the woodsy aroma. 'I had to meet someone.'

'Your mistress?' She moved away from him.

He could tell by the tightness around her mouth and eyes what the question had cost her. She had not taken the time to change out of her wet clothing and she looked exhausted, worse than this afternoon.

'No. Before we discuss this, and we need to, will you please get out of that wet dress and into something dry? I don't want you getting an inflammation of the lungs when I need you to nurse me.'

Her face turned mutinous. 'I am tired of you telling me what to do all the time. I will change when I am good and ready. As for getting sick, it would serve you right if I did and Burroughs had to take care of you—or Roberts.'

He sighed. 'You are the most stubborn woman. At least come over here, where I can see you better and the warmth from the fire can reach you.'

She edged closer.

He finished the whisky and poured another glass. Dutch courage. What he had to say to her was not going to be easy. He had never said this sort of thing to a woman. He hoped it was not too late.

'I went to see my mother.' He waited for her reaction, dreading that she might feel disgust for the woman who had birthed him.

'Your mother? I thought you hated her.'

'I thought I did. I don't know any more.' He stood and went to her. Putting his hands on her shoulders, he asked, 'Are you happy with me?'

'What kind of question is that?'

She looked wary, as though she expected him to say something that would hurt her. He knew he had made her feel that way by his actions. He had kept her at a distance.

'This is not easy.' He released one of her shoulders and held his hand out. 'See, I am shaking.'

'That is very likely from your wound and all the whisky you have consumed,' she said drily.

His mouth twisted. 'You are not being very helpful.'

'I did not know I was supposed to be.'

'It would help.'

She eyed him speculatively. 'I don't think I want to help you. Remember, you did not help me when Papa caught Emily and Prinny.'

'That was between your father and stepmother. This is between us. And you are not happy with me anyway,' he finished for her. 'You thought I was unfaithful.'

Juliet nodded. A sense of dread weighted her down and her stomach was a tight knot. Was he going to tell he had a mistress, as she suspected? How cruel.

'Don't say anything else,' she said hastily. 'I don't want to hear any more.'

He caught her chin and made her look at him. 'I have never been unfaithful to you,' he said solemnly. 'I have not been with another woman since you burst into my life on the duelling field.'

Juliet stared at him, not sure she had heard correctly. She swallowed the lump that had lodged in her throat. 'I...I—'

'Don't believe me,' he said bitterly. 'I never thought I would regret my past, but you are fast making me do so.'

He abruptly released her and went to the window, his back to her. She staggered before catching her balance.

'I don't understand,' she said, her voice barely above a whisper.

'Neither do I,' he said, sounding as though the words were dragged out of him. 'I thought I had everything under control. You are a woman, and women cannot be trusted. I was going to stay faithful until I got you with child, then I was going to go my own way and let you do the same.' He turned to face her, a haunted look in his eyes. 'But I can't. The thought of you with another man tears me to pieces.'

Her mouth dropped.

He gave her a wry smile. 'Amazing, isn't it?'

'What are you saying?' She held her breath, hoping against hope.

'My mother told me everything tonight. About her being pregnant with me when she married the Duke. How he hated her for it and treated her badly. Everything. It gave me a lot to think about. Especially about us.'

She took a step towards him, but stopped. She did not know what he was really saying.

His smile disappeared. 'Come here.'

'Why?'

She knew that if she went to him and made everything easy he would never finish what he had started. Or so she told herself when she held back. She wanted him more than anything. But she would not be hurt by him again. She could not go through that.

'You don't trust me,' he said.

'You are the one without trust,' she said sadly. 'You made that clear from the beginning. You told me that you have no mistress. I find that hard to believe, but I am willing to do so because you tell me it is so.' In her heart she added that she was willing to believe because she wanted so badly for him to belong only to her.

'I know. And I am still not sure. Not completely.'

She bit her lip to keep from saying something she would regret later. 'Then perhaps it would be better if I left for a while.'

Leaving him would be the hardest thing she had ever done but if it would give him a chance to decide what he wanted she would do it. More than anything she wanted their marriage to work. Having him love and trust her would be heaven, but if he could not do that she would settle for his companionship. She loved him that much.

He came to her and wrapped her in his arms. 'No. I want you to stay with me. I am just not sure that I can give you everything you deserve.'

She kept her head lowered, not wanting him to see the need in her. His words, that said so much but not enough, left a bone-deep ache in her chest.

He stroked her hair, tucking a loose strand behind her ear. 'I have not trusted a woman in a long time…since I was ten and learned what my mother had done. Yet she came back to explain everything to me, things I had not been willing to listen to before. She told me not to take my bitterness and distrust out on you. She made me think.'

Juliet began to shake.

'Don't,' he said, stroking her back. 'I don't want to cause you pain.'

She nodded, her head rubbing up and down on his chest. She still refused to look at him.

'I wanted you from the beginning. At first it was physical and…curiosity. I had never met a woman like you. Then it was more. I could not stand the thought of you being hurt.' He took a deep breath.

'After we were married, it was more. I wanted to make love to you all the time, and when we were apart I wanted you by me, just to be near.'

Tears started to seep from Juliet's closed eyes. She was so anxious about what he was saying, what he was going to decide.

'I want you to stay with me, Juliet. I don't know for sure if I love you, but I want you. I am not sure that the two are not the same.'

She slowly slipped her arms around his waist. It felt as if she had longed to hear those words from him all her life. 'I love you so much, Sebastian, it is a constant ache.'

'Then look at me,' he said. 'Tell me to my face.'

Taking her courage and determination in both hands, she angled her head back. 'I love you. I think I always have.'

'Ah, Juliet,' he murmured, bending down and kissing her.

It was a sweet melding of flesh. Desire was there, but it was like a banked fire waiting to flare to life later. They could wait. Right now they were committing themselves to one another.

When the kiss was over, she gave him a tremulous smile. Tears still seeped occasionally from her eyes. Only one thing remained. As much as she did not want to ask, she had to know about trust. Without it their love would not last. That much she knew.

'What about trust, Sebastian? Do you trust me? Can you?'

He groaned. 'You cannot leave well enough alone, can you?'

She shook her head. 'No. If you don't trust me, then what will happen to us? You will forever torture yourself, and consequently me, with your doubts about me and about our children.'

His arms tightened around her. 'I know. That is what I have wrestled with all night, and I cannot answer you for sure. Trust is too new. I want to trust you, but I fear there will be times when I slip. When I hurt you with my lack of faith.'

'Oh, Sebastian,' she whispered.

'But I want to try. If you will give me the chance.'

She heard the doubt and longing in his voice. 'I don't think I can live without you. I am willing to try with you to make this work. I know it will not be easy, but I want to be with you.'

'Juliet, my love,' he vowed.

Epilogue

Twelve months later...

'Sebastian,' Juliet called, 'what are you and Timmy doing? Your mother will be here any minute, and you know how she dislikes not seeing Timmy.'

The Duke and a baby with a head of peach down came out from the dining room, where they had been for the last hour. Sebastian handed the boy over. 'I think he needs changing.'

'Oh, no,' Juliet said, crossing her arms. 'You can take him to Nurse as easily as I can. And you had better hurry.'

'I will call Mrs Burroughs,' Sebastian said with a wicked gleam in his eyes.

'No, you will not,' Juliet said, humour tipping up her mouth.

Sebastian gathered a gurgling Timothy close with one arm and pulled his wife in with the other. 'You are a stubborn woman, my love.'

She grinned up at him. 'And you are a scoundrel, always trying to foist the unpleasant aspects of parenthood off on me.'

He returned her grin. 'The boy is the spitting image of you, therefore you should be the one to do the nasty things.'

The smile left her face and she paled. 'He is your son, too.'

Sebastian's eyes darkened and Timmy squirmed. 'I am sorry. I told you it would not be easy, but that was a year ago. I know these past months have not always been the bliss we could have wished, but I don't doubt Timothy's parentage. He is mine and yours. No one else had a part in his creation, and I believe no one else will have a part in the begetting of our next children.'

'I would not trade them for the world. But are you sure?' she asked, doubt still a tiny kernel lodged in her heart.

'Yes,' he said. 'Now and for ever.'

Joy replaced the disquiet. She clung to her family with an intensity that she knew would increase with time.

'I love you, Sebastian.'

'And I you, my love.'

Timothy, caught in the middle of his hugging parents, laughed in sheer delight.

* * * * *

MILLS & BOON®

Makes any time special™

Copyright © Harlequin Enterprises Limited 1997
All rights reserved

Mills & Boon publish 29 new titles every month. Select from...

Modern Romance™   **Tender Romance**™

Sensual Romance™

Medical Romance™   **Historical Romance**™

MAT2

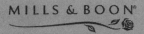

MILLS & BOON®

Historical Romance™

HIS ONE WOMAN by Paula Marshall

The Dilhorne Dynasty

Jack Dilhorne was in Washington DC on business when war broke out between the North and South states. It was not the best of times to meet someone as intriguing as Marietta Hope. And their mutual enemy seemed determined to keep them apart…

THE VEILED BRIDE by Elizabeth Bailey

A Regency delight!

Why does Anton, Lord Raith, need to advertise for a wife? Rosina Charlton feels her pulse race as she walks down the aisle towards the stranger who is to become her husband. Has Rosina committed herself to a man who wants a marriage based on convenience alone…?

On sale 2nd February 2001

Available at branches of WH Smith, Tesco, Martins, Borders, Easons, Volume One/James Thin and most good paperback bookshops

0101/04

2 FREE

books and a surprise gift!

We would like to take this opportunity to thank you for reading this Mills & Boon® book by offering you the chance to take TWO more specially selected titles from the Historical Romance™ series absolutely FREE! We're also making this offer to introduce you to the benefits of the Reader Service™—

- ★ FREE home delivery
- ★ FREE gifts and competitions
- ★ FREE monthly Newsletter
- ★ Exclusive Reader Service discounts
- ★ Books available before they're in the shops

Accepting these FREE books and gift places you under no obligation to buy, you may cancel at any time, even after receiving your free shipment. Simply complete your details below and return the entire page to the address below. *You don't even need a stamp!*

YES! Please send me 2 free Historical Romance books and a surprise gift. I understand that unless you hear from me, I will receive 4 superb new titles every month for just £2.99 each, postage and packing free. I am under no obligation to purchase any books and may cancel my subscription at any time. The free books and gift will be mine to keep in any case.

H1ZEA

Ms/Mrs/Miss/Mr ....Initials......................................
BLOCK CAPITALS PLEASE

Surname ....

Address ....

....

....Postcode..............................

Send this whole page to:
UK: FREEPOST CN81, Croydon, CR9 3WZ
EIRE: PO Box 4546, Kilcock, County Kildare (stamp required)

Offer valid in UK and Eire only and not available to current Reader Service subscribers to this series. We reserve the right to refuse an application and applicants must be aged 18 years or over. Only one application per household. Terms and prices subject to change without notice. Offer expires 31st July 2001. As a result of this application, you may receive further offers from Harlequin Mills & Boon and other carefully selected companies. If you would prefer not to share in this opportunity please write to The Data Manager at the address above.

Mills & Boon® is a registered trademark owned by Harlequin Mills & Boon Limited.
Historical Romance™ is being used as a trademark.